MW01126971

ALIEN HYBRIDS & NYMPHS OF JUPITER

ALIEN HYBRIDS & NYMPHS OF JUPITER

A NOVEL

LOU BALDIN

ALIEN HYBRIDS & NYMPHS OF JUPITER

ISBN: 9781076226112

Independently published

Contents

January 20, 2019

PROLOGUE

Lying is the only truth on Earth. The only truth that humans understand and accept. Without lies, there is no religion, no science, no politics, no trust, no love, no courage, no heroes, and no virtue. All those things are based on lies.

Conversely, the only truths are those most ridiculed as absurd by the general population and scientific minds of Earth; Extraterrestrials, the paranormal, and the reality of Nymphs in everyday human life, however unknown and unseen by the vast majority of humans.

Truth is despised by most humans because truth demands everything of us and leaves us empty shells. The truth is that humans are EXTRATERRESTRIALS existing in a paranormal reality awash in pixies. The truth is that there is no such thing as "To go where man has never gone before." Humans have been all over this solar system this galaxy and this universe at one time or another. Humans have been everywhere during one of their thousands and even millions of incarnations.

Most manifestations happen on utopian planets where souls in various levels of spirit and physical form live blissfully. On the flip side, a sizeable portion of souls exists in subpar planets and realities, stuck in the reincarnation cycle of bliss and pain for some and only pain for others. There is hope for those in Hades (Earth), and millions of souls escape the reincarnation merry-go-round and enter stable and pleasurable utopic realities in due time. Enter the Hybrid world one of many destinations after death.

CHAPTER 1

COSMIC ASSIGNMENT

My name is Michael Bolderini, and I have been given a task by Milton (An Extraterrestrial from a distant star system going by the pseudonym of Milton). Should I choose to accept the assignment, all I had to do was reply with a "yes," and telepathically, Milton hears my answer and responds.

Sometimes I do, and sometimes I don't take assignments offered by Milton due to the nature of the beasts involved and or time constraints owing to my own endeavors and responsibilities here on Earth.

I accepted this latest assignment because it intrigued me and mirrored similar past projects that Milton asked me to take on that I enjoyed doing. But more so, I accepted the job because Milton promised me a surprise that I would appreciate should I choose to take the mission.

Soon after accepting the assignment, I'm surrounded by a horde of small critters, leprechauns, goblins, trolls, fairies, elves, pookas, spirits, ghosts, and Gnokki, or some such interdimensional paranormal lollygaggers. Mythical creatures that have haunted humans on Earth for centuries but now exist in the fictional segment of libraries.

Mythical creatures are presumed to be figments of wild imaginations found in drunkards, drug addicts and the insane. Or are classified as legends, folklore, fairytales that irrational adults and perfectly normal children believe in. Sensible people never see such things. Therefore, such things don't exist. Rational minds need not read any further.

Gnokki is a name I came up with to describe strange paranormal little critters that did not fit into the category of all the other known ghouls and goblins. The word "Gnokki" in the context of this book denotes the singular and plural vernacular of the creature(s).

The Gnokki have powerful abilities that change three-dimensional reality into a maze of multiple dimensions in a blink of an eye when dealing with humans. Gnokki is a creature(s) that often manifest during "Alien" contact or abductions, and the first things wiped from people's minds when the contact ceases. Gnokki performed the mind-wiping themselves when they are involved in transactions during abductions and sometimes during and after friendly encounters.

Abductees, for the most part, have no clue that interdimensional beings exist and are hardly able to grasp and describe exactly what it is they have encountered that has left them distressed, frightened, confused, and often pissed off.

It is not only the Gnokki and other paranormal subliminal hobgoblins that create voids in human thought processes, and patterns, disrupting the human mind. Greys and other intergalactic beings in charge of the abduction operations dabble in mindwipes too.

Gnokki specialized and focus their primary activity towards human/Alien Hybrids and not so much with ordinary humans already plagued with a plethora of cosmic mischief makers in their daily lives. Each situation is different, and the Gnokki decide how much influence and interface they conjure up in the minds and bodies of those placed into their possession, however temporary that possession.

Gnokki are the ones that landed in my office and surrounded me in preparation for my immediate departure. Other creatures in the regiment with the Gnokki remained subtle, and out of my full awareness, yet part of the posse sent down to procure me and take me to Milton.

In a flash of light and a crackling sound of an electrical sounding whip, followed by a strange metallic odor that filled the air, I'm instantly inside of Milton's ship. Others were on the ship before my arrival. A mixture of humans and humanoid guests, victims of mysterious Alien tampering and plagued by creatures oozing from crevices and pores from the innards of the ship.

"What's with all the drama, Milton?" Slipped off the tip of my tongue as I found myself once more inside

17

the belly of an intergalactic flying circus of interstellar magnitude.

"Why don't you beam me up plain and simple, Milton?" I asked.

"It is plain and simple from my perspective, Michael. It's the human perspective that sees the drama, the ugly, the monsters and alien creatures, and critters. The things that are sometimes a mixture of reflections of the souls who see them and are hints of past lives and experiences... don't you know that, Michael?" Said Milton.

"Of course, it is, Milton," I responded with a cynical tone.

"Make yourself at home, Michael, and I will get back with you shortly." Promised Milton.

"Will do, Milton," said I. Fully understanding and aware of the fact that Milton's time schedule is as unpredictable as the weather in my part of the world.

Making myself at home while at home inside my house is doable and pleasurable. But while inside of an Alien ship, a zoo filled with endless probabilities and possibilities for 3D mind pulverization, followed by relentless criticisms from Milton and his crew, not so much.

Nonetheless, I forged ahead into the ship's mysterious interior, which is dark and gloomy at first but brightens considerably as I proceed towards the belly, the soul of a spaceship that has more life in it than all of humanity on planet Earth combined.

Milton's ship is alive, a living breathing thing existing far beyond human comprehension or rational description. The Gnokki, the strange cosmic critters that showed up in my home office moments before I was whisked up into Milton's ship, traveled separately from me and were not with me when I initially arrived on the ship, that I could tell. Gnokki seemed to be interdependent parts of the living ship, fragments of the ship's mind and soul if the ship had such.

Some of the Gnokki remained behind in my office in my house, where my wife, Debbie, was sleeping in her bed and probably dreaming of sugarplums dancing and so forth, and unaware of the terror that was now roaming freely inside our abode. I wasn't given a chance to warn Debbie of the Alien invasion having been snatched up and taken, abducted by Aliens (Gnokki), and stashed inside of Milton's domicile posthaste.

Had Debbie known about the Alien critter infestation, she would have been mortified, terrified, shrieking, and running for the hills, as any normal human would under similar calamitous Alien-invasion conditions.

Debbie and I, like so many married couples nowadays, slept in separate bedrooms because of one or the other, if not both, snores in their sleep or make other rumbling distracting sounds. Debbie snores, and I'm a light sleeper, which makes sleeping in the same room dubious. Not that I sleep much anyway and end up wandering in the house like a specter in vain attempts to be productive.

I normally tinkered with things in the basement or worked in my office on the computer long into the night, writing manuscripts and answering endless questions on emails, personal messaging, and various internet forums into the early hours of the next day. While Debbie sleeps soundly in her bedroom, unaware that I'm not in bed snoozing away as she.

Sometimes I'll take a short nap right before Debbie gets out of bed or go for a long walk in the neighborhood or at a nearby park with a walking trail to "while" away the time (kill time). Debbie is used to the fact that I could be sleeping in my room, and scarcely ever looks in on me not wanting to wake me, aware of the difficulty that sleep presents for me.

Debbie knows that I occupied some of my time out in the yard, weather permitting, working in the garden, or building something or other in the front, or the backyard.

Debbie kept busy with her own things, crafting in her craft room, making fanciful cards for every occasion, and giving them to family and friends. The bottom line, we seldom see each other during the day or night other than at mealtimes sitting in front of the big screen, our large and thin LED television during the dinner hour. It is a near-perfect relationship and living arrangement, we didn't get in each other's hair much. We are both retired, old, and sometimes grumpy.

The critters that didn't remain in my house but beamed up shortly after I did, dispersed and vanished into Milton's ship ahead of me clearing the way, a path for me or setting a trap. There was never a way of knowing what cosmic creatures were plotting or doing until the trap snapped shut.

Spontaneously, I received pieces or crumbs of information once I was inside of Milton's ship but not enough to have all the gory details of the who, what, and why they were even there, the critters, the Gnokki, and for what purpose they served this go around.

Routinely, a few of the Gnokki were garrisoned, sent down into my house to watch over the place while I was gone, taken into the mysterious realm of the cosmic abyss until my eventual return to planet Earth. But what other things the Gnokki did around my house I was never sure about. Milton always vague with his answers when I asked him for specifics concerning the vagabonds infesting his ship and my house.

Milton's ship interior changed constantly and remained in a state of mutability, continually altering colors, shapes, sizes, and sounds. Therefore, it was disorienting and impossible to remember where the furniture used to be at any given moment to give me perspective and orientation from past visits on where to report.

Making oneself at home when the decor was never the same required moments to acclimate and familiarize once more to the bizarre nature of Milton's ship. A near impossibility and a huge challenge for humans stuck inside a 3-dimensional reality for any length of time, as was I... and other abducted humans invited last minute to the party.

That morning, moments before Milton's abrupt interruption into my life, the weather was cold as ice, which was falling from the sky in sheets. Sleet and snow drifting and blowing and swirling chaotically pushed and pulled by howling winds made visibility bad and seeing out my window difficult. I was at my computer catching up on loose-ends that needed to get done, and the clock on the wall displayed 2 AM.

I got up from my chair and walked over to the window where frozen rain was hitting hard against the glass in the form of tiny ice pellets and tapping out a winter melody. I wiped away condensation and saw nothing going on in the street in front of my house other than the rapid accumulation of snow and ice.

Normally a minimum of traffic flowed even at this early hour of a January morning due to the fact my street was a designated snow route and promptly cleared of snow when inclement weather hit.

Every so often, snowplows barreled down the road creating a racket loud enough to wake the dead.

Unsurprisingly, Debbie slept through the noise and commotion.

I was glad Debbie slept through it all, considering the circumstance that unfolded that morning, with no advanced notice from Milton and his band of cosmic hoodlums, who happened to be in the neighborhood and decided to drop in on me.

Snowplow blades scraping against the hard surface of the road made annoying noise like large fingernails scraping across a large chalkboard, a most aggravating racket. Sleeping on my street is never easy when winter weather brings out the snowplows during nighttime hours.

Meanwhile, above my house and hidden from view due to the blinding snowstorm and the murkiness of night hovered Milton's Alien ship, his UFO, my cosmic ride for the next few hours if not days. If days, my doppelganger (clone) would be activated to take my place at my house while I'm away.

Debbie never suspected during previous times when Milton whisked me away, and my body and soul lugged to faraway places, other than when she jokingly said to me, "where's that 'other you,' dear, I miss him." Debbie's way of letting me know when she feels the affection in our marriage waned. A conundrum husbands and boyfriends around the world experience frequently, I suspect. It makes me wonder if my doppelganger is making moves on my wife when I'm away on cosmic business.

I walked into one of the many rooms inside Milton's ship, the room I was asked to report to for further instructions by Milton after being summoned by him. Inside that room was not Milton but a bizarre freak show, a circus of strange, funny looking animals bouncing off the walls, the ceiling, and the floor with the energy of 3-year-old children on sugar-highs, a categorical madhouse.

The creatures were not the Gnokki that came down into my house that morning and bustled and escorted me up into Milton's ship. What was in that room was far more inexplicable and creepier than the creepy and unfathomable Gnokki.

A few of the critters were milling about and smoking odd-looking cigars that emitted a cloud of dark noxious gas that seeped out of various orifices on their heads and bodies. The critters looked like a pile of leaves about to spontaneously combust.

The gassy fog emitting from them saturated the room with a sticky, disgusting looking, and smelly residue that obscured my view and affected my vision and my ability to reason and think clearly. I was momentarily drawn into a fog of mind reminiscent of an acid trip I took many decades ago while in the army. The smoke was powerfully repugnant, or perhaps the creatures were powerfully repugnant, it was an appalling smell, and I didn't linger in that section of the ship long.

The animals in that room were nothing like caged creatures found at human zoos or those running free out in the jungles in the wild. They were alien beasts of types I hadn't seen before or in a while or have forgotten about, perhaps blocked from my mind by Milton or other Aliens like him.

I've seen my share of freak shows inside of Milton's ship through the years and, therefore, not surprised by some of the amazing and grotesque lifeforms that often showed up out of the mist from hidden compartments and dark recesses and obscure niches. The animals were of various sizes, shapes, colors, and smells with nasty inhospitable attitudes that could inflict fear into a pack of lions.

Milton chimed in and said, "The critters are a type of ogre menacing the humans on my ship today and every day when humans are on the ship. Ogres acting like sheepdogs corralling the humans to proper places in the ship."

Having heard that from Milton, I surmised that such creatures took on different forms and shapes and even attitudes and represent that part of the crazy ritual that abducted humans are forced to endure during Alien abductions.

"Rituals that make humans' skin crawl with fear during regression therapy. For those abductees who seek out regression remedy while attempting to figure out what the hell they been through. Such mazes of contrived realities are blockades hiding what really takes place." Said Milton.

Milton continued his sermon, "Regression typically discloses little of the reality behind the reasons for abductions. Crafted and made up scenarios are designed to obfuscate and keep hidden the true nature of Alien encounters."

Milton was not in the room that I could tell or remember. Although, I would not put it past Milton or be surprised if he were one of the animals in the freak show that jeered at me the whole time that I was traversing that small space where time slowed to nearly a stop. It was like walking through molasses. Milton didn't make himself known during that morass nor answer my queries but made off the wall comments as usual for him.

The creatures didn't talk to me or give me much lip as some Alien creatures I've encountered in the past have, but they managed to get my attention and to respect the cosmic powers they owned.

It was like meeting with the local Don, a mob boss back in the old hood where I grew up. You had to get through a line of sharply dressed shady characters heavily armed and capable mafioso soldiers who wouldn't hesitate to slit your throat and dump your carcass into the Missouri River (at the behest of the Don). It was a dangerous morass to get to the Don for a friendly chitchat.

The beasts in the lobby of the ship were disorganized and looked like broken teddy bears or other types of nightmarish fractured ripped apart monsters that someone did a sloppy job stitching back together, but their powers necessitated respect, as did the local Don.

Inside the room a few doors from the "lobby" with the smelly and deranged creatures, the room I was supposed to go to but apparently took a wrong turn due to the furniture rearrangement, was three women, two were standing, and one was on a surgical-type metallic-looking table.

The woman on the table was knocked out (asleep) while two Grey Alien beings were busily implanting fertilized eggs into her uterus, or something of the sort. The two other women standing nearby the table where the woman lay were conscious but not fully aware of where they were and looked confused and tired having been taken from their comfortable beds and dragged into this ship earlier that evening, hours before I boarded Milton's ship that morning.

The two women were not panicked, they seemed calm and unafraid, which were signs of having been drugged by the Aliens and now in a mellow state of mind, enjoying a tranquil and peaceful visit on Milton's ship.

The women were clothed in undergarments, one in panties without a top and the other with a top and no panties. The woman on the table was stark-naked, and her scant bed clothing removed from her by the Aliens was lying on the floor nearby the table.

EXPEDITION BEGINS

Milton's ship drifted slowly from above my house moving further into the night sky and then shot like a pixy through the clouds and into space in a blink. I was able to view the happenings outside the ship from a small floating device, a monitor gizmo that began following me from the moment I entered the ship, and kept me informed of pertinent occurrences (more or less) of the happenings in and outside Milton's ship. The device alleviated Milton from having to give me blow-by-blow descriptions of things that were happening around me and within the ship.

After Milton's ship reached space and broke away from the gravity of the Earth (the subsequent happenings had nothing to do with leaving Earth's gravitational field), other types of beings made their visual presence known to me but made no comments or attempts to communicate with me initially. The Alien beings were in telepathic contact with the two women, and they took the women who were standing nearby the surgical table to another place inside the ship; for reasons, I was not told until later that day.

The naked woman on the surgical table then woke up and was groggy and confused and began to vomit on herself and onto the floor of the ship. The vomit did not float around the cabin but fell to the floor of the ship and splattered into a disgusting lumpy puddle of green gunk.

One of the creatures, bots that were standing sentry inside that room, and near the surgical table, activated and speedily went over to her and cleaned the vomit from her body and from the floor with a suction apparatus that emerged from the bot's body. A Grey alien came into the room and helped the woman off the table and got her dressed in the clothing (a plain tee-shirt and nothing else) that she originally had on when she was abducted earlier that morning or late the previous evening. The woman did not see me standing nearby and was led away by one of the small Alien creatures to some other room on the ship for further processing.

Keeping track of "Aliens," what they looked like, how many there were, and what types of species they are is not possible for a human mind while on an Alien ship. It was difficult to discern the goings-on in the ship, and for me to achieve any kind of accuracy of who and what was on Milton's ship at any given moment (things changed constantly) even with the information monitor following me around and Milton's occasional quips.

During my briefing, on-the-fly that morning with Milton or a facsimile of Milton, things came at me in rapid-fire succession. Milton had not completely left the ship and phased in and out of my conscious view while he explained my duties for that day. Through that time, other Alien creatures raced by me so fast they didn't even leave an imprint on my mind. Of what they were or what they did or why they existed, and for what purpose they were on the ship, I would never know.

Milton clarified for me only what he believed essential for the moment and placed the rest of the flurry of information into my subconscious mind for later retrieval.

The two other women who had previously been taken away had already been implanted earlier with fertilized Hybrid eggs by an unknown being/creature (sperm donor) inside the ship before I arrived that morning. I learned that from the floating device following me.

As I stood in that room unsure what I was there for, another female was brought in, and her clothing removed by two of the Grey creatures and piled on the floor next to the table. She had more clothing on than the previous three women had on.

This woman, Meg, was her name, was fully dressed as if she was ready to go out shopping or out on the town when she was abruptly abducted. Meg wore blouse and slacks, with a long wool sweater that covered her down to her ankles. Meg had a prominent protruding potbelly that she couldn't hide under her long flowing loose-fitting sweater. Meg looked pregnant.

The Grey creatures that brought Meg into that room stood about four feet tall and displayed similar mannerism, composure, and appearances as if they were carbon copies of each other and cloned from the same egg... or whatever contraption that constructed them.

The identical twins, the two Greys, were comical mimicking each other's moves and dancing around the room and around Meg as if they were rehearsing for a part in a theatrical production and not taking their jobs seriously. It was comic relief for me but not for Meg, who was unconscious of everything happening in the ship around her.

Keenly amused by the two Aliens clowning around, I almost lost it and cracked up in laughter, but with great effort, I managed to remain composed, not wanting to draw attention to myself by bursting into hysterical laughter. The woman, Meg, that the comedic Greys brought in with them and playfully danced with was oblivious of the Grey's and their silly antics and to the fact that she was on some godforsaken Alien vessel and being pranced around like a show horse by the two Greys.

In the room, besides the comedic Aliens, Meg and I were a few highly intelligent bots (Alien robots) as the one that cleaned up the puke moments before. The bots remained stationary and nearly invisible until they were triggered into action by some need that propelled them out into the open to perform whatever tasks they had to perform.

The number of bots and various other paranormal critters in that room and on the entire ship only Milton knows, but due to the noise and confusion being generated, there had to be a crowd of them. An invisible hidden in the background horde that I could not see but could hear the low-pitched sniggering.

The worker bots had uncanny perfect human speech patterns and verbal capabilities, sharp intellect, and manners when they chose to be polite. The bots could and did communicate telepathically and verbally with the women on the ship and me. The bots could be rude and menacing as hyenas and be all over you and get in your face for no understandable reasons.

Humans encountering the bots and fully aware of them would not believe the bots were robots but something extremely bizarre and dangerous as hell. The bots were not real mechanical robots or physical, fleshy creatures either, but something otherworldly and incomprehensible to humans.

To their credit, bots are extremely effective and efficient performers concerning whatever they engaged in. There are several species of bots with various temperaments, some more placid and not as aggressive as others. Bots, as I discovered during that day, displayed other annoying habits besides aggression.

Bots jabbered vocally and loudly in perfect English amongst themselves or whenever two or more of them activated for reasons unknown as they did in the delivery room.

Bots spoke all the human languages. When foreigners are abducted and processed, and communication called for, bots did the interpreting for the interested dignitaries on the ship.

Turning bots off or getting them to shut up was not humanly possible and potentially hazardous for those who tried. Abductees are tranquilized from the moment they are picked up until released on their return to their bedrooms and are never aware of the bots and their incessant blabbering. I had to bear the noise and confusion and muddle through it. Mercifully, the chattering ended when their work was completed, and they shut themselves off, went invisible, and hid in the many crevices, small slits inside most of the rooms in Milton's ship.

Meg was calm while the two Grey creatures removed her clothing and prepped her for the delivery of her baby. Meg was ripe for giving birth at any moment. Meg was not distressed but peaceful due to a drug, a fluid, administer to her by one of the bots using a syringe device that emerged from the bot's body.

Soon after the Greys placed Meg's naked body on the metallic table, gadgets erupted from the ceiling, dropping down all around Meg and caging her inside a mess of dangling wires, cables, and metallic, dark but glowing iridescently and mysteriously, rods, bars, or shafts.

Meg's body then elevated up off the table and floated in mid-air held by an invisible forcefield created by the effervescent rods. This was a natural birth for Meg, I was told, without the use of drugs or mechanical stimulation to force the baby out of Meg's body, regardless that the birth looked highly mechanized to me. The drugs Meg received earlier that morning were to induce amnesia to block out the happenings inside the ship from her mind and had nothing to do with the birthing process underway.

One of the Greys touched Meg's belly with its finger or some inert device the Grey was holding and instantly induced "natural" labor. As Meg's baby slowly slid down from the birth canal and out of Meg's womb, Meg moaned and screeched with intense pleasure. Meg experienced an immense orgasm, one of the most powerful orgasms she ever felt in her life. While Meg cringed in ecstasy, the baby floated next to her, and Meg grabbed the child and held it to her breasts.

"Giving birth is the big Kahuna of orgasms, unlike any orgasm a woman can have. Few women on Earth experience overwhelming pleasure because humans complicate things and don't do "natural" correctly as the creators of nature and human bodies intended. The orgasm is for mother and child and creates a cosmic bond between them that lasts indefinitely. The intense orgasm is the soul merging with flesh and an important element for the healthy development of the body and soul of those involved." Whispered the Gnokki into my ear.

"The father initiated the birth with Meg six months earlier during lovemaking with her. His soul-based orgasm blasted the physical sperm with a high dose of spirit radiation that left an imprint of his soul in the flesh of Meg's egg, which became impregnated, became alive, and in this case, became a Hybrid human." Said the Gnokki.

After a short time passed, the Grey took the child from Meg and placed the baby on a small floating tray that was next to Meg, where the baby was cleaned by the Grey. The Grey used an assortment of gadgets that swirled rapidly around the child, leaving the baby spotless. Nevertheless, the baby wailed and cried during the cleaning process and the furious handling by the Grey creature.

The rods and cables then withdrew back up into the ceiling and out of the way. The umbilical cord was not cut, and the mother and child were reunited for a time. The baby fed on the mother's breasts while still connected to the umbilical cord. The umbilical cord was left attached to Meg and her baby the whole time the child was with Meg.

The woman, Meg, is human. Her baby is not. Meg did not seem affected by the strange child nursing from her breast. Meg acted as if it was a natural thing a normal birth with a normal human child. Meg was not aware of me or the Alien creatures attending her or that she was breastfeeding a strange entity, not of the human world.

Meg's mind was blocked of the reality she was going through, replaced with a projected scenario manifested by an ET Alien being that kept itself hidden in the background inside of Milton's ship, and running the whole show while out of sight and out of human mind.

I could see the tall Alien orchestrating things in the ship, like a conductor conducting an orchestra because he allowed me to see him. But no communication took place between us.

The conductor was a tall man with human facial features and a male physique. He was cleanly shaven, had black hair that was trimmed, not long and flowing. His dress was casual, shirt tucked inside slacks, and men's loafers for shoes. His appearance was totally unexpected by me, and he looked borderline geeky. The thought, "what the hell," went through my mind, and I immediately suspected that he must be Milton.

Reading my mind, the man said, "No, I'm not Milton." "And I'm not the projected image you see."

I left it there. I assumed if Milton wanted me to know about that conductor, Milton would tell me more about him. The Gnokki said nothing about that man either.

Meg was infatuated with her new baby, joyful and excited about the birth of her first child. Meg was a single woman age 25 with a college degree in finance and worked as a loan officer at a bank near the house where she lived. Meg dated men but had no boyfriend or a relationship presently and was impregnated by one of her encounters from a party that she attended approximately six months earlier (this Hybrid species had a six-month gestation period, not the typical nine months that human babies endure).

Meg didn't know the man who impregnated her. But had her suspicions of who he might be. Meg decided not to tell him about her pregnancy and the baby wishing to sever, cut off the short and awkward relationship with the man she hadn't seen for weeks after her one-night stand with him.

It was a chance encounter at a drunken party with some of Meg's girlfriends at a local bar. Meg considered having an abortion but decided against it and planned to raise the child on her own. The decision to keep the child was implanted in Meg's mind; otherwise, Meg would have aborted the child due primarily to her circumstance and her not being familiar with the father of the baby.

After some minutes passed, the Aliens moved Meg, and her child into another room where Meg continued for a time to nurture and bond with the strange baby. The bonding was done primarily for the child's benefit and not so much for Meg, who would not be allowed to raise the Hybrid child that she gave birth. The child could not survive in the Earth's environment while inside its Hybrid container. The Hybrid child was designed to live on other types of planets and moons and inside Alien ships like this one, which accommodated Alien-Hybrid physiology and human physiology.

About an hour after giving birth, Meg was taken back to her apartment, where it would appear to her that she suffered a miscarriage, and the birth episode on the Alien ship blocked from her mind. The ship was no longer in Earth's orbit, and Meg was taken back to her residence on one of the planets and moons in this star system from where humans were abducted, using another Alien vessel with the other three (or more) women.

The Hybrid child remained on the ship placed inside a nursery with other Hybrid children that had recently been harvested from human females from various parts of the star system, including from planet Earth. Meg was abducted from Earth.

Meg and the Hybrid child continued to see each other regularly inside of this Alien ship or others like this ship where they would be allowed to interact as parent and child a few hours during each visit approximately once a month for the first year and then no more until the hybrid was fully matured. The child would remember the visits subconsciously, and the human mother, Meg, would too on a subtler context than the Hybrid child.

Meg would live out her life unaware that she had a living child, believing that she lost the baby, and had come to terms with that manufactured reality relatively quickly with the help of the Alien beings forever involved in her reality.

Hybrid children were not distressed when mothers were taken away from them. Hybrid lives are filled with a maze of distractions that Hybrids are immediately immersed in. Unique activities for each child created by the nannies who cared and provided for the Hybrids from birth to maturity.

After the Hybrids reached their temporary home via Milton's ship, on one of the many moons in the star system, their upbringing became increasingly complex and comprehensive.

Hybrids received uploaded instructions and learning directly into their minds that fit their future individual and unique requirements and agendas. Also, Hybrids received one-on-one training by multitudes of ET creatures during their existence, creatures that entered Hybrid bodies and minds and influenced the Hybrid's mental and physical status and capabilities.

Gnokki had a peculiar interest in the Hybrid babies. Gnokki appeared in the nurseries with strange toy-looking gadgets and devices that they used to amuse the Hybrid children. Hybrids in that nursery varied in ages up to 2-year-old toddlers.

Other women had given birth on this ship before I had entered that morning, some moments earlier, some weeks and months earlier, and the nursery/play area was teeming with Hybrid children. I counted 24 in the one nursery I visited, but there were other nurseries on the ship that I didn't need or bothered to visit. The mothers and sperm donors of the children in the nursery had been returned to Earth or other planets and moons before I came on the ship.

Hybrid babies and children developed quicker and more rapidly than human babies and children, both physically and mentally. Most of the Hybrids in the ship were up and running around the room, playing and chasing each other with the vigor of older, more mature human children under similar circumstances.

The caregivers on the ship, the nannies, and the bots had their hands full with taking care of the extremely energetic and feisty Hybrid toddlers. Gnokki instigated and provoked the children into playing strange games with them, which set off a battle with the nannies that pushed back to keep the Gnokki from meddling with the childcare routines. Gnokki avoided the bots but teased the easily exasperated and passive non-aggressive humanoid nannies.

Bots held their own against the Gnokki and treated the mysterious and provocative Gnokki as hostile intruders. It was amusing and confusing the cosmic creature squabbles considering they all resided in the same ship and are elements and sovereign extensions of Milton's ship.

Gnokki were not intruders but part of the Hybrid edification education squad assembled and tasked by higher beings as caregivers to the Hybrids. The Gnokki are perplexing and always an unknown force when measured against the other mysterious lifeforms as the bots.

Gnokki had additional duties in other places that took up their valuable time, and they showed up infrequently in the nursery. Gnokki provoking the Hybrids with bizarre methods and Alien devices and other objects contributed to the Hybrid's rapid physical growth and cerebral evolution.

CHAPTER 2

JUPITER'S MOON 891

The ship's destination was Jupiter's moons, one of its far-flung moons named 891. The ship circled moon 891 and morphed into a unique geometrical shape that conformed precisely with an opening in the moon, and in an instant, the ship permeated through the surface of that rocky moon. The ship entered a massive city structure several hundred feet below the moon's rock-strewn surface.

The city lacked modern buildings and vehicle traffic, as found in most cities on Earth and many other places in the star system. The city was not primitive but deficient of contemporary conveniences that are abundantly available on nearby moons, planets, and space cities. Grocery stores, theaters, shopping centers, and other human dispensers of necessities and distractions didn't exist on moon 891 because the city was not designed for human occupancy. The city was formulated like an ant hive with tunnels and passages and rooms small and large that went on seemingly forever in every direction in a maze of webs, layers, and strata.

Ships as the one I traveled in were the prominent vehicles inside moon 891 and one of the types able to penetrate the combination lock (security system) to enter the solid surface of that moon. A steady stream of similarly classed ships came and went carrying human and Hybrid cargo to places, planets, and moons confined to this star system.

I was unaccompanied by other humans, traveling alone, the only human on the ship except for the tall human-looking Alien who claimed he was not a human. There might have been humans tucked away in any number of the hidden niches, crannies, and rooms on Milton's ship, but I was not made aware of them. All the abducted humans had been returned to their beds on whatever planets/moons they were taken from before the ship arrived at this location.

My itinerary entangled me in several anomalous projects that day that I had yet to get a full grasp on how or when they were to unfold. Milton failed to mention that Gnokki and other interesting critters would follow me around like meddlers that fazed into and out of my wispy reality, for the duration of my assignment. I realized quickly why the nannies agitated easily by the Gnokki and their less visible cohorts that imposed themselves on the Hybrids in the nursery. Gnokki involved themselves in every detail of every situation like dust in a windstorm gets into every niche and cranny.

The moon city is a Hybrid repository, a Hybrid detention center, a foster home, a cosmic orphanage all in one, a place where Hybrid children are stored while they age and mature like a fine wine.

The city is attractive, not dark and mysterious but lively with ongoing activities for Hybrid youngsters to lose themselves in loads of unadulterated fun and fantasy. Children and their nannies could be seen everywhere in the city, along the nature trails and the mysterious colorful and glowing passageways and tunnels oozing with delightful and intriguing interstellar ambiance. A jolly place where juvenile Hybrids going about their routines and playful practices unperturbed by the myriad of strange creatures and human types like me from other ships and residents, in their midst.

No day and night intervals "inside" the moon only daylight and daytime all the time.

Moon 891 is a playground, a funhouse overflowing with entertainment, enjoyment, and development created to distract Hybrids until the moment of individually prearranged maturity happens.

Nannies are a mixture of humanoids; some are female Hybrids, physical beings with human qualities and characteristics, and mechanical robots (bots). The bots and nannies are under constant supervision by the tall Alien being, the humanoid, or one like him. He remained in the background and in another room like a mainframe supercomputer humming and buzzing and occasionally

44

giving off a dizzying array of strobing and blinding light. Each ship had its own similar contraption running things.

The tall Alien coordinated and manipulated the processes and aspects of ongoing situations in various rooms in the ship systematically and wirelessly (telepathically and other such means). The mysterious and subtle tall beings are stationed in places humanoids frequented, and one or more of them are stationed or garrisoned on moon 891 and performed similar duties as they did on the Alien ships (run the show).

Bots varied in height, size, and baffling abilities triggered by where they are located and stationed, which moon, or space city or Alien ship assigned to and what they are programmed to do by the tall beings supervising those facilities.

Bots and Gnokki didn't mesh and had conflicting traits and approaches and seldom cooperated, like oil and water. Gnokki were smaller than bots, shorter than two feet in height, and most Gnokki are less than a foot tall but shapeshifted often.

Gnokki horsed around with the Hybrid children, who loved the attention and perked up when Gnokki showed themselves. Bots chased the Gnokki away, protective of the Hybrids who were easily swayed by the transient unmanageable and often invisible Gnokki.

Bots are even-tempered sometimes, hostile other times, and could detect the Gnokki even when invisible.

Gnokki are prone to vengeance and had the advantage, the upper hand in most skirmishes, but knew when to back off.

Disputes were comical when Gnokki took revenge on the bots in amusing, entertaining schemes like clowns pranking each other at a circus.

Circus clowns are paid to act and create entertaining gigs and comedies. For the Gnokki, it was their nature and approach to doing things to distract, foil, and achieve ultimate goals. Gnokki were not acting. They weren't trying to be funny or entertaining around the bots, only outmaneuver the bots.

When Gnokki weren't annoying in their sleight of hand maneuvering, they were hilarious critters. Gnokki made me laugh with their ingenious and intense antics. I didn't mind when the Gnokki entangled themselves with other specters on the ship, the moons, and the cities we journeyed to. Distracting escapades kept the Gnokki busy and out of my hair and out of my head, but never for long.

Bots took Hybrid children to unknown places deep into the bowels of moon 891 for extended coaching sessions where temporary tangible "software patches" for lack of a human term, were inserted into Hybrid brains; Hidden places where whatever happened to the Hybrids would be known only to the bots and the Hybrids tinkered with.

Information was stored inside Hybrids' subconscious minds for release at scheduled future times when Hybrids were paired with a soul and a destiny.

Undisclosed assignments given to the bots by the tall beings are designed to frustrate tampering with the Hybrids by illicit spirit beings that managed to infiltrate and attempted to insert rogue souls into the thousands of empty vessels that the soulless Hybrids are.

Rogues are akin to squatters who move into empty houses that don't belong to them. Squatters are discovered and ejected eventually, but worth it to them the short stay inside a living Hybrid body, until they find another soulless Hybrid body to squat in.

Bots, under the control of the Tall Beings who showed up or showed themselves occasionally to the Hybrids and other sentient beings, used the bots to sniff out squatter souls.

Duties ascribed to the bots involved caring for the Hybrids and disciplining in similar techniques as human children. Bots are the parents that Hybrids don't have.

Atypical to how human children are cared for on Earth, Hybrid rearing is intensified and infused with supernatural abstract elements involving nymphs. Human children only receive the storybook fairytale versions of the nymphs, or so, humans believe.

The palpable enchantment that is Hybrid lives is the lure, the attractive lifestyle sought by renegade souls rather than the difficult life on inferior planets like Earth, where hardship rules over mind, body, and soul.

Bots are limited in their abilities to root out the "various" invader souls that crop up like new viruses in a never-ending cycle. The ragamuffin souls developed ways to fool the bots by blending in with the soulless Hybrids and not giving themselves away by acting "alive," "activated" into living fully aware Hybrids with a soul.

Gnokki are not fooled by the scheming "lost souls" and can go deep into the subconscious minds of the Hybrids and find and eradicate squatter-souls that don't belong. Gnokki chewed up the squatters and spit them out, literally taking bites out of the soul's lifeforce-hide and leaving them scarred and tagged.

In this sector of moon 891, the approximate ages of Hybrid children ranged from birth to 17 years. Separate fully-grown Hybrid camps in other parts of the moon housed 18 to 35-year-olds.

Age had little bearing on the Hybrids concerning maturity or knowledge levels. Selected Hybrids didn't age past 18 earth-years per stipulations in their contracts. Some Hybrids continued to age up to 35 and no older per prior arrangements.

The age Hybrids reached was programmed into them at birth, by the Tall Ones in attendance at selected moments after each Hybrid's conception and subsequent formation in the womb.

Personalized preset know-how and knowledge are uploaded into Hybrid brains by numerous beings up until the predetermined adult age, and then Hybrids with souls and without souls are ready to be shipped to utopian colonies.

Hybrid children are courteous, respectful, and obedient, to the point of being robotic towards each other and the nanny-bots and other instructors that molded Hybrids into what they become.

Gnokki played the wildcard in the creation process and introduced mischief and bedlam for the Hybrids to trick out hidden residual contaminants from body and soul. Such impurities seeped into the turbocharged Hybrid Minds during and throughout the scope of each Hybrid's grooming. Gnokki stirred the pot for a short time, injecting elements that spiced up the normally intense and serene atmosphere cycle of Hybrid development.

Things calmed down in the childcare institution when the Gnokki left the premises of the nursery, and the Gnokki left when I left. The Gnokki seemed attached to me by some invisible cosmic tether lassoed to me the moment I entered the ship that morning. Several similar teams as the Gnokki and I worked in the Hybrid camps around the clock and managed to remain out of each other's crosshairs.

Gnokki existence is a mystery, and outwardly such types of creatures tagged along with humans and created a buffer zone around their human cohorts for the mutual protection of humans and the things humans come in direct contact with while in the cosmic unknown.

The many types of bizarre creatures and critters that work with the Hybrid's development in plain view and those deep behind the scenes/curtains always out of view are a considerable and indecipherable potential hazard to humans.

My Milton-provided outfit (clothing) gave me adequate defenses and advantages for most situations existing in the places I traveled to in the cosmic region. Additionally, the Gnokki provided backup and failproof coverage from unforeseen creature-perils easily encountered by those traveling through space. Gnokki constructed barriers to shield me from various forms of cosmic radiation designed to blunt unwanted space vermin and unauthorized spacefaring humans, which are many.

Equally, human bodies are a jumble of contaminants and carriers of numerous pollutants that are bad for Hybrids in the early stages of development. Humans shed hair, skin, gases, and abundant other biological particles that sicken some types of nonhumans with conflicting viruses and microorganisms. Nonhumans and other creatures, bots, nannies, Gnokki, and critters hidden from view contaminate areas they occupy with copious bodily impurities, and anomalous cosmic pollutants picked up from galactic travels, that affect humans and others physiologically and psychologically (body and mind).

HYBRID CITY

The Hybrid city in the bowels of moon 891 is constructed of an organic plastic composite material that covered the city in colorful florescent moss. The material radiated a glow that provided substantial illumination without light fixtures or sunshine. The temperature in the city remained at 78 degrees, which radiated from the composite material like the old-style steam radiators in antiquated buildings back on Earth.

The interior of moon 891 is amalgamated interwoven metallic organic plastic common in utopian zones. The complex Alien substance covered the walls, ceilings, and floors, and supported a matrix structure that accommodated plant, animal, and Hybrid life seamlessly.

Hybrids did their business freely like animals in the forest and at petting zoos and, as the wildlife in nature, do. Hybrids are one of the many inhabitant creatures running loose, wild, and free within the forest city. Hybrids dropped pellets and urinated onto the porous ground that absorbed the waste rapidly and is a far superior and efficient system than the one that exists on planet Earth concerning recycling nutrients back into the soil. The ground is covered by edible vegetation that the animals and the Hybrid children fed on like grazing cattle.

Small goat-like creatures romped and leaped about like Mexican jumping beans among the Hybrids, mingling and playing with the Hybrids and feasting on the same vegetation growing throughout the forest town.

Hybrids had a future purpose that linked them directly to their human biological parents, the females that gave birth to them, and the Hybrid males who contributed semen that impregnated the human eggs.

Hybrids born on Alien ships, like the one that ferried the fetuses and toddlers to moon 891 and other moons, were brought to this city or one of many similar facilities and kept, stored, and incubated, until needed by the DNA donors. Not for body parts; however, such things were commonly done by other agencies in conjunction and accordance with human/Alien initiatives in the star system, mostly by Alien Renegade species deficient in proper biological resources.

The sexual orientation of Hybrids is male, female, and sexless eunuchs. Regardless of sexual orientation, all Hybrids in utopia are sterile, they cannot reproduce even as adults.

Hybrids played amongst themselves and occasionally hibernated in caves and niches throughout the city whenever they felt the need to sleep (seldom) or burn off energy, which is all the time. Hybrid children have a much higher vitality level to deal with than human children and would be considered impossible to deal with in human-type classroom environments and situations. Hybrids had no restrictions or requirements as sitting in school rooms and did all their learning and living on the run while interacting with numerous instructors and a plethora of nymphs.

Instructors applied sophisticated uploading techniques to infuse information directly into the Hybrids' brains without the hardship and boredom of learning by repetition as is done in the human world.

Hybrid children are not sexually active while living inside the city and only became so when they are fully initiated into a permanent place of residence on other moons and space cities destined to be sent to.

Genetically, the child Hybrids produced hormones that kept them in good working order and with accommodating pleasurable moods for the duration of their incubation periods.

Hibernation was lengthy, often lasting weeks and sometimes months just before full maturity when Hybrids readied themselves to leave the nest, the nursery. Children, regardless of age or sex, slept together, huddled and cuddled in clusters directly on the soft grass and the hay they helped gather from the fields.

There is no rhyme or reason for the duration of the hibernation periods, and children came and left the hibernation huddles as they pleased, individually before graduating to other cities. Hybrids are naked and kept warm by the controlled temperature throughout the city and from internal body heat generated by hyperactive hormones. Body heat generated by Hybrids was a bit higher than that of humans on Earth, roughly 99-101 degrees.

Lakes, ponds and running streams of pristine, pure, clean potable water provided Hybrid children refreshing drink, and swimming and bathing opportunities, which are leisurely and uncrowded considering the large numbers of Hybrids residing in that section inside moon 891.

Plants and trees (flora) sporadically grew in some areas and are dense brushy forests in other places in the city.

The forest vegetation harbored and sheltered assortments of tame wildlife (fauna) and magical insects as butterflies and other creepy, crawly critters that the children interacted with, played with, and then sometimes if not always, ate. Insects are tasty and nutritious and a large part of the Hybrids' diet.

Nannies are a combination of humanoid two-legged creatures and freaky multi-limbed octopus-type beasts that scurried to and fro feeding hungry toddler Hybrids wherever they happened to be.

Gnokki detested octopuses, miffed by the freakish multi-limbed beasts lumbering around and not communicating or interfacing properly with the Gnokki for guidance and intentions. The Gnokki vanished, left the area whenever the octopus-creatures came near, or lumbered by and disturbed the Gnokki's frolicking with the

Hybrids. Land octopuses have multiple tits for several children to feed on at once like that of a sow.

Above is a picture of a sow feeding its young someplace on Earth. Pictures of bizarre milk-machines with multiple arms lined with tits (land octopuses) on moon 891, currently unavailable.

The weird milk-machine creatures scampered in the city, providing convenient and expedient nourishment around the clock anywhere in the village where Hybrid children are burning off their immense stored energy.

Land octopuses turned into puss-like blobs when they fully bloated with milk and scurried off in search of suckling Hybrids to defuse their swollen bodies and tentacles. Milk was generated and created when the beasts fed on the abundant vegetation that covered the city ground with succulent multicolored flora.

Milk-producing blobs pulverized the grass and other vegetation into a pulp using four rows of embedded razor-sharp rotating teeth, always in spinning motion in the mouths of the lactating machines. The octopus blobs had more than one mouth, three or more openings depending on the size of the creatures. The bigger blobs are sluggish, moved slow and remained on the surface of the city, whereas smaller blobs are nimbler, swifter, and searched out the underground niches and tunnels where Hybrids frolicked and played.

The freakish milk-producing creatures had nothing in common with the lactating dairy cows back on Earth, which produced cow's milk and not human milk that was fed to humans. The octopus blobs produced milk from mammary glands equal to human mother's milk and formulated specifically for each individual Hybrid in the moon city based on the Hybrid's biological mother's milk.

Human babies could not stomach Hybrid milk. The milk corresponded to that of the human mother and a fertile Hybrid father's specific genetic code, a created mixture specifically formulated for each Hybrid child.

Milk-producing-blobs are fearsome-looking but not formidable or harmful. Blobs moved like miniature tanks mowing through vegetation that encountered the machine-like orifices gobbling up bushels of grass and leaves at a time. The land octopus-blobs were gentile as kittens as long as Hybrid fingers and Gnokki stayed away from the toothy grinders of the ferocious multi-jawed milk monsters. Still, the creatures are not a danger to the Hybrids or the Gnokki, who are immune to most hazards.

No set mealtime existed on moon 891 or anywhere in the utopian colony. Hybrid children ate and fed whenever they had the urge, which was all the time, as is true with healthy human children if they are allowed to eat all the time, they would. DNA kept obesity and illness away, and the children are wholesome (fit as a fiddle) the whole time they lived in the village, and for the duration of their existence until decommissioned after serving a primary purpose.

Hybrids would not remember their time growing up in the Alien nursery, memories are blocked the moment the Hybrids are relocated to a new residence.

"The village (nursery) was enclosed, hidden inside the moon where the distant sunlight could never reach or penetrate. Nevertheless, the city was well lit and bright in the park areas where children played and interacted the most with each other and the nannies." I often heard such information whispered in the background that I periodically picked up like a weak radio signal, a random noise with bits of information mixed in. I mistakenly presumed the sporadic chatter came from Milton and said so in a loud voice:

"That's a lot of rambling, Milton," I said in a clear audible voice, hoping Milton would respond.

Milton chimed in, "That noise is not coming from me, Michael, but from the Gnokki. Gnokki are the narrators that interpret and relay information to those around them during assignments. Gnokki dispenses information both verbally and telepathically based on situations, conditions, and with whom they are transmitting the information. Gnokki have done that sporadically and subtly since the moment you accepted this mission, Michael. It's their job keeping you informed until the end of the mission."

"I didn't think it was you, initially, Milton, but never thought who else it could be. Which of the four Gnokki is the chatterbox? They all look, act, and sound identical."

"The Gnokki are multipurpose creatures and have one foot in the physical world and one foot in the supernatural world at all times, Michael. The Gnokki are part of my ship, a minor part. The Gnokki operate individually or as one. Therefore, anyone of them or only some of them or all of them have invaded your space and sometimes your brainwaves, Michael." Said Milton.

"By the way, what is that urgent question you want me to answer that keeps popping up in your head, Michael? Noise and incessant chatter are going on where you are, and I didn't make it out. I'm a long distance from where you are and receive a lot of static...from you."

Before I could give Milton a smartass answer, Gnokki droning and chattering kicked in again and much louder (intentionally to drowned out my grumbling).

"Inside the nooks and crannies and caves, the lighting was dimer allowing for the children to sleep or hibernate for as long as they wanted. The city was sealed, lacking openings and passageways to the outside of the moon to keep unwanted intruders out. The only way in and out was through the Alien space machines, like the craft Milton allowed you to travel inside of today. Many similar flying machines came to and departed the city routinely around the clock, even though there are no clocks or any need for knowing the time." Said the mysterious voice coming from one, some or all the Gnokki.

I took advantage of the pause from the Gnokki and asked Milton my burning question.

"Milton, are we, me specifically in real-time or am I in one of those time cube mishmash screwy time deals that humans get twisted up in knots when inside of them?"

"The illusion of time is always a mishmash no matter where you are, Michael, even while on Earth, as you should know by now. Hurry up and spit out your question before the Gnokki muck up the airwaves."

As little children do when adults are talking, pay no mind, and jabber on as if the person you are talking with doesn't exist. That's how the Gnokki roll. Gnokki knew that Milton and I were talking and ignored us and prattled on. However, the Gnokki have helped keep the peace between Milton and me by censoring and tampering my gift for sarcasm.

"Millions of Hybrid children and their retinue of attendants inhabited the city and maintained a consistent population that seldom increased or decreased by any significant numbers. New Hybrid children are added, and many departed the city in continuous streams of spaceships that ferried Hybrids to and from the moon to other points of interest. Those departing are relocated to places, planets, moons, and satellites within the star system. Some for the duration of their existence and some until they are taken out of the star system to other stars in the Milky Way Galaxy." Said Gnokki.

"Selected Hybrids voyaged to other galaxies in the universe to serve at the whims and desires of their predestined masters who owned them body and soul," stated the Gnokki.

I got a word or two in edgewise:

"Milton, back when I first entered your ship this morning and was introduced to your zoo of weirdo, eccentric and peculiar crew, then watched helplessly as women were stripped out of their skimpy underwear and alien contraptions inserted into various body orifices and then had to view a woman give birth… All that nauseating stuff and I hadn't had my morning biscuits and coffee yet, which most likely was a good thing, or I might have barfed like that one woman did…" Said, I.

"Stop right there! Michael, is this going to be a long whiny session rather than a simple question? If so, I'm turning you back over to the Gnokki!" Bellowed Milton from afar.

"Damn! A bit grouchy today? Milton." I Said.

"Ok, Milton, my question is, I spent a little time in one of the nurseries on your ship this morning, not because I was interested in seeing a bunch of newborn Hybrids burping, farting, and pooping, I just happened upon that room that turned out to be a nursery. Anyway, one of the baby Hybrids winked at me. It couldn't have been a few hours old or perhaps a few days old. At first, I thought it was the lighting in the room or trick of my imagination typical of being inside a rabbit-hole Alien ship, as your ship is. I walked up near to its container crib thing, and the baby continued to wink at me and smiled. The Hybrid didn't look more than a few days old at most."

"And what's your question? Michael."

"I have seen that same Hybrid child inside moon 891 during my walk this morning, but she is now about ten-years-old if not older. She winked and smiled at me again but said nothing. I tried to talk to her, and she ran away."

"Yes, Michael, that is the same Hybrid girl and a conundrum, and I don't want that to interfere with your assignment so back to work, and I'll get back to you on that later."

CHAPTER 3

I had in my possession a handbag with cosmic powers that could shake heaven and hell (Earth) to the very core with the mystical contents inside of it. But I wasn't sure which was more mysterious and perhaps more powerful. The handbag, the strange critters, the Gnokki that clung to me like needy toddlers, or the menacing gremlins that haven't communicated directly but scurried around like field-mice into and out from behind the cosmic curtain perhaps clearing a path or obstructing it.

"A human psychiatrist would have a field day with this information, Milton."

"Yes, that's why aviator pilots and astronauts keep their mouths SHUT about the strange things they see in the skies and in space, Michael. And those that do talk about UFOs and "Aliens" seldom if ever mention the freakshow of ghouls and goblins (nymphs) that menace them, specifically because of the straight jacket they would find themselves knotted up in if they talked about such things. The personal invasion by so-called mythical nymphs usually goes to the grave with those who experience them. So, don't go blabbering about nymphs, Michael."

"Whatever you say, Milton, no blabbering. I'll only write about it in my journal and then add it to my growing book collection."

Thinking out loud knowing Milton is listening, "The handbag, the strange container of cosmic material from what dreams and nightmares are made of that you gave me soon after I entered your ship, Milton, didn't come with much instructions from you before you vanished. What is in it, and what do I do with the contents? The Gnokki have remained quiet about the handbag too. Not much has remained unmolested by the curiosity of the Gnokki, nor their innate desire to explain every detail about everything, except the handbag."

Rhetorically speaking and not expecting an answer from Milton. I've had many one-sided conversations with Milton and other superior beings who love to remain quiet and divulge little as possible about much of the goings-on in the universe.

Gnokki tended to get into everything, every nook, and cranny of the ship and of the places we traveled, even inside the minds and bodies of the Hybrids and my mind too. The Gnokki's abilities to morph into animals, insects, people, and inanimate objects like trees, bushes, and plants as they had while in the nursery on moon 891, baffled me.

That morning, soon after I entered Milton's ship, I left my wallet, car keys, pocketknife, and a few coins sloshing around in my pockets, inside my locker on the ship. I exchanged my street clothes for a special robe, garb that was in my locker, and placed my clothes and shoes there to be retrieved at the end of my journey.

In the locker was an assortment of footgear/shoes and sandals with a bunch of other tantalizing strangeness that I didn't bother or have the time to investigate further. I chose one of the pairs of sandals because sandals are what I wear year-round even during the winter months while home on Earth, for comfort.

I exchanged my Earth sandals with the cosmic sandals in my locker. The sandals have unusual qualities that I noticed immediately after placing them on my feet. I was able to levitate and flow around the ship a few inches above the floor. The sandals moved higher or lower off the surface, or I could simply walk if I had that in my mind to do. No learning curve or balancing act required on my part. I zipped around the ship like a pro the moment I strapped the sandals on.

The robe, sandals, and the handbag provided me with extraordinary abilities and shielded me from cosmic hazards and certain types of beings that existed in the places I was to visit during my assignments.

Hybrids had bodies designed and equipped for the extremes of the places they would be sent to live. I didn't have the innate protections without the garb from the locker and was going to the same places the Hybrids were going.

The locker is stuffed with items and gadgets that I would retrieve when needed during my assignment period. The locker was not the walk-in locker that I own in the cube city near the sun but paranormally connected to that locker.

The ship operated under Milton's discretion, and he created the unique program it would operate during that day. Milton chimed in every so often and told me that there are others on the ship that assisted him with the chores, and they remained in the background out of the way and mostly out of sight and mind. Milton was not on the ship after the brief encounter when he handed me the handbag and said he had other things to do and faded out of my view.

I was an observer for much of the trip with a few duties sprinkled in along the way, which became apparent the moment they needed implementing. Sharing information with others was unacceptable during assignments, and therefore, information was not triggered into my mind for application until then. Afterword, the fulfilled act having been carried out and accomplished evaporated from my brain, leaving few details about my involvement.

Memories used to describe much of my assignment of that day, this day, in this book are skewed and tangled but close enough for the mishmash existence the physical world runs on. Notwithstanding that, "close enough" counts only in horseshoes, hand grenades, and government work, and now this report.

Milton advised me that the Gnokki were my secretaries for that day and kept track of every detail of my assignment and would share some of that information with me when appropriate and that I didn't need to put info into my mental journal or my leather-bound journal. Soon after, Milton said that the Gnokki confiscated my leather-bound journal and scrambled by mental journal and provided the distilled information in this book.

JOVIAN CITY

One of the Greys on Milton's ship alerted me that the ship was taking on the last batch of Hybrid cargo (children) and would soon depart moon 891. The Gnokki should have given me that information and would have had they not gone off to pout after a misunderstanding when I suggested they tone down the redundant speechifying emanating from them like a leaky faucet. They accused me of being pissed for taking away my journal, which I was.

When alerted by the Grey, I was in the forest city leisurely exploring the many fascinating places, locations, and sites unescorted by the locals, which I appreciated that they didn't tag along and breathing down my neck during every step I took. I received the message from the Grey from an orb display that continually changed shape and was about the size of a baseball that hovered above me and remained with me wherever I went. The orb kept track of my movements without breathing down my neck... I did swat at it a couple of times to no avail.

Obscurity at any level is impossible anywhere in the universe. Humans on Earth have no idea the level of cosmic surveillance occurring every second of every human life on the planet by celestial beings (nymphs). Roughly 8 billion human souls are monitored 24/7, which is a pittance compared to all the souls in the star system, mostly under similar scrutiny.

Milton-classed ships had the same wormhole, Stargate time and place shifting abilities as the pods, and folded space-time into zero time when traveling through cosmic fibers of illusionary matter.

The Grey sent a pod to my location, and I entered the pod and was taken back to Milton's ship instantaneously, or so it seemed with its ability to manipulate time. The Gnokki, having picked up on the message, somehow managed to find me and decided they would crowd into the pod with me without asking if they could come along. I was a considerable distance from the ship at the time of the call, but the pod made distance a non-issue like walking through a portal and finding my physical self at my destination. Pods also had capabilities for scenic tours when large distances were not involved.

Milton-classed ships had the same wormhole, Stargate time and place shifting abilities as the pods, and folded space-time into zero time when traveling through cosmic fibers of illusionary matter.

Many human theorists have speculated and believe that places on Earth have hidden static, stationary, Stargates strategically placed in various places on planet Earth. They believe the Stargates were created by extraterrestrial civilizations in the past and that are now long gone or extinct (the Alien civilizations). And that powerful world governments (superpowers) have gone to war over such "Alien" mechanisms and phenomenon and used war as an excuse, a cover, to capture and subdue peoples, regions, and nations harboring Stargates.

The theorists are wrong. Stargates are not stationary and located in godforsaken backward countries. Stargates are mobile and exist inside of Alien ships (UFOs).

And are plentiful all over the planet, the moon, and everywhere in the star system where Alien ships reside. Humans have limited use of stargates, and they are only allowed to selected agencies and a few VIPs by the covert overlords of planet Earth.

While I was exploring moon 891 on foot, and gliding inches off the ground with the power of the sandals, Milton's ship had left the nursery city and ventured to other places on that moon without me. Milton's ship traveled to other similar cities and sites inside moon 891 to pick up older Hybrids and other humanoids for transport to other cities and places in the star system.

I had disembarked from Milton's ship soon after the ship arrived on moon 891 early that morning. Milton's ship penetrated one of the large caverns below the surface where the nursery-city resided. Several cities existed inside moon 891 and are separated from each other inside various cavities like in a pomegranate with its partitioned caverns and spaces.

Inside moon 891, filled with ripe seeds (Hybrids) segregated from other batches of seeds; Hybrids, humanoids, and humans too, ready for picking, packing, and shipping to client cities in the Jovian region.

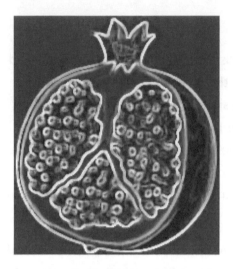

Pomegranate

Moon 891 resembles a compartmentalized pomegranate with its separated sections that contained Hybrid tykes (children) and matured Hybrids ready for harvesting. Sections for other types of humanoid, nonhybrids exist on moon 891 also that had nothing to do with my assignments, and therefore I didn't explore or visit those restricted sections of the moon and have no information about the inhabitants and goings-on.

MEMORY IMPLANTS

During my stay inside moon 891, I shared items from inside my Handbag with some of the Hybrid children that I encountered along the paths and tunnels and on my list for tampering with. Unbeknownst to them, the Hybrid children, I pressed items from the handbag directly into the back of their skulls/heads as they passed me on the trails, or I passed them.

I first sprayed a solution onto the area of the skull, where I was to insert the objects to prepare the spot for fusion. The solution made the bone soft and malleable like putty, and the objects easy slid into place inside the skull, and then I covered the hole with the malleable bone that I pushed out of the way temporarily to make way for the thing inserted. The bone stiffened quickly and healed in seconds, leaving no trace of entry or swelling on the skull.

Some Hybrids grabbed their heads momentarily as the mild pain from the implant shot through them. The pain was brief and didn't linger long. Other Hybrids didn't even notice and showed no reaction to the implants that I pressed into their heads. I did the same to several of the children during their sleep and hibernation periods, which made the procedure easier for me and no pain for the Hybrids while they snoozed. The Hybrids were unaware of my presence or that I existed and carried on with their carefree routines as I hovered around them in stealth mode made possible by the magical sandals and Alien garb.

I was invisible to the hybrids when I interacted physically with them and became nonexistent due to the clothing I wore from my locker in Milton's ship. I made myself visible to them when I completed my duties, and whenever I needed face-to-face contact. The nannies and other caretakers knew I was there, having been alerted by the Greys on the ship of my assignment in that city, which the caregivers were accustomed to and prepared for.

The Gnokki dispersed in every direction the moment the ship landed and managed to regroup with me the moment I received the message to leave the moon. The Gnokki never explained what they did on that moon other than visit with some of the Hybrids and surrender personal information to the Hybrid children unique to each Hybrid child.

Much about the intent of the Gnokki unfolded, and I became aware of it as it happened and when they let me know what they did. Gnokki were chatterboxes and loved to give me reams of information that jumbled up most of what they were telling me. Part of their scheme to create confusion and distraction to hide most of what they were about and what they truly were doing.

I seldom communicated with the nannies and the other creatures in the city employed for maintenance and labor, nor with others who were doing what I was doing. "No need to mingle with them or anyone else and divulge secrets not for sharing with anyone." Reminded the Gnokki.

None of the Hybrid children received the same things, items, inserted into them by me, or the uploads from the Gnokki into the Hybrid brains. Each item I inserted was specific to each Hybrid child and not cookie-cutter for all the Hybrid children.

The Handbag harbored infinite types of items designed and crafted for each soul and soulless Hybrids. Many of the Hybrid children in the city had no souls inside their skulls (brains). Hybrids without souls were the ones the Gnokki and I were interested in most. However, Gnokki found reasons to interface with many of the Hybrids with souls.

I allocated additional time with the Hybrid that winked at me back on the ship that morning, she had aged rapidly and was now the equivalent of 14 Earth years. I named her Tam. I didn't insert anything into her brain as I had done with many of the other Hybrids on moon 891. I was puzzled that she was able to acknowledge me because she had no soul and incapable of much awareness other than the basic puppy-love alertness that all Hybrids without souls had.

I eventually learned from Milton that the Gnokki penetrated Tam's mind, and they were the ones winking at me from inside her Hybrid head. Milton didn't explain why the Gnokki did that other than there was a reason for it.

Tam was not ready for the upgrade but was on my schedule for other things. The Gnokki were inside Tam's head, making some of the finishing touches in preparation for an upgrade.

I was flabbergasted at how fast Tam was growing and maturing practically right before my eyes in one day. That super-rapid growth wasn't the case for most of the other Hybrids that I was aware of. It was obvious that some tomfoolery was going on, and I was not on the same page as Milton and the Gnokki.

Many of the Hybrids I had placed objects into their heads were complete and prepared to move to permanent stations in the utopia colony without further processing and would be taken to their residences by the Greys inside of Milton's ship or other similar ships. Some soulless Hybrids that reached maturity are taken to utopian cities and roam with the animals and undergo further upgrades while there.

Soulless Hybrids received unique experiences, memories that allowed them a depth of reality, a constructed reality that had bits and pieces derived from real-life memories from other sentient beings. The memories served a larger purpose that opened at a future prescribed time when the Hybrids relocated to transitory residences. Most residences are transitory, impermanent, temporary.

I was one of several Handbag carriers dispensing cosmic wonderland stuff, goodies, trinkets, and other interstellar objects and much more that will remain hidden if not divulged in future chapters of this book.

The Gnokki brought with them dreams and memories, created memories by the Gnokki themselves, and real memories and nightmares too from past lives that the Gnokki snatched at some point from god-only-knows-where and uploaded the memories into the empty minds of many of the soulless Hybrids. Not all the Hybrids were tampered with or upgraded. They were too young and years away from maturity or are defective.

Milton said there were other reasons besides lack of maturity that certain Hybrids remained on the shelf and out of commission, inoperable, broken, but he forgot to elaborate on the reasons and whether the affected hybrids would be repaired and placed back into service at some point.

Milton claimed he told me about the defective hybrids but then wiped the memories because I had no further reason to know or carry that info in my mind, beings it was not part of my assignment.

I pressed Milton further on more information about Hybrid Tam, and why she was growing like a weed and the other Hybrids not so much. Milton replied that other Hybrids were also rapidly developing, not all but some and that I hadn't taken notice for lack of interest in them. That was true, so much was happening that morning that in a real-world scenario would have taken decades to unfurl and come about. Milton manipulated time and crammed a bunch of stuff into the space of one day.

Dispensers of cosmic products, which I played a small part, didn't congregate, socialize and exchange information, jokes, talk trash or spread rumors, and gossip about the cosmos. Seldom did we cross paths, and when we did, we kept going without even sharing a "hello," "good day," "how's it going?" or "goodbye."

"It wasn't important or necessary to indulge in small talk or any talk," advised Milton.

This was not my full-time job more of a fluke, as it was for some of the handbag transporters and handlers and their entourage of cosmic paranormal critters that tagged along with them. For me, it was a glance at the goings-on behind the physical world that Milton existed in; An opportunity to see the machinery in action that runs like clockwork in the unknown cosmic reality where so many endless billions of souls reside.

Most souls exist in magnificent spender living in utopic worlds and realities while at the same time on the other side of the cosmic tracks, many souls live in desperation and barely getting by on lower level planets. A wonderous reality is hidden from the vast numbers of humanoids in the lower end of the totem pole where humans are trapped and entangled in backward beliefs and ego-driven delusions. Nevertheless, some humans with minimal awareness levels are enraptured by life itself even with the grain of sand grasp on life; however, few they are.

Hybrids are peerless, and each has unique realities and exclusive awareness of the cosmic world around them, even when in the same place and surrounded by the same things.

CHAPTER 4

UTOPIA COLONY

After departing moon 891, Milton's ship neared the planet Jupiter on its way to other moons of Jupiter. The ship made frequent stops along the way, picking up and dropping off Hybrids and other pertinent creatures that would accompany the Hybrids' to new realities.

Gnokki would be some of those elements that entwined and become part of Hybrids' new existence. Gnokki inserted parts of themselves into the Hybrids' bodies and minds weaving into the Hybrid DNA fibers the wisdom of the universe, selected parts of it, prescribed by higher spirit beings, per each Hybrid.

Hybrids are peerless, and each has unique realities and exclusive awareness of the cosmic world around them, even when in the same place and surrounded by the same things.

Food tasted differently, colors are perceived differently, smells and touch, and sexual acts, too, are unique to each Hybrid. No two Hybrids perceived the world they existed in the same way as the others.

Hybrids are never on the same page about anything other than language and, even then, existed variation in grammar.

When talking with each other, Hybrids discovered tantalizing perceptions of other Hybrids, which created fascinating conversations about what and how other Hybrids viewed unique-to-the-individual, concepts.

Hybrids are spared the torture of politics and religion and societal pretext, beliefs, and views and all types of negative ideas and impressions that perturb humans. Hybrids cannot become "more enlightened" other than what is already programmed into them at the moment of full activation into the utopian colony.

My next destination after moon 891 was a vast colony hovering above Jupiter. One of the thousands of similar colonies with many cities, drifting above, below, and in the clouds of the Jovian planet.

Jupiter is a planet of ungodly stature and unimaginable beauty. Jupiter's massive proportion took up the whole visible spectrum as I traveled inside Milton's ship towards the multihued flamboyant planet of the gods.

Jupiter is stupendously gargantuan and mind-numbing spectacular from every angle attainable from Milton's ship. Jupiter could easily hold 13 to 14 hundred planets the size of puny planet Earth. A number incredibly difficult for a 3-dimensional mind to comprehend when Earth itself is extremely huge and not puny at all from a human perspective.

After Milton's ship arrived at its preprogrammed destination, I jumped ship, having inserted myself inside the one-man plus, pod given to me by the Grey Alien. The Gnokki again blew my 3-dimensional mind and shrunk down in size and inserted themselves, all four of the Gnokki, into my handbag soon after they boarded the pod with me.

Plenty of room in the pod for them in their current size without them becoming shrinking violets, but they didn't ask and did as they pleased. I was glad they did; Gnokki are not always a barrel of laughs, far too technical, and mostly rambling amongst themselves ceaselessly in a perplexing language.

Nevertheless, Gnokki are multitalented, godlike, incredible at multitasking, gracious, and accommodating at times. Gnokki can distract the Hybrids while performing delicate precision mental upgrades on Hybrid brains and internal biological machinery (body parts) without the Hybrids aware that anything is happening to them. Gnokki tweaked and made necessary adjustments to the finished product (Hybrids) before I inserted items from my handbag into the Hybrids and before Gnokki inserted their own unique and specialized items into the Hybrids.

ROMAN GOD

Jupiter was more than a gas giant as viewed by the intellectual, scientific minds back on planet Earth. Jupiter, besides being known as the Roman God of the Sky by ancient Romans is a moon-producer and so much more that can't be covered in one small book, hundreds of books, perhaps, would scratch the surface.

Jupiter, over the billions of years of its existence, added thousands of moons, moonlets, and other bulky debris as comets, asteroids, space rocks, and dust into the star system and ejecting the same beyond the star system and into the darkness between the stars.

Jupiter is a multifunctional cosmic mega factory used by numerous sentient entities roaming and residing in the star system. Jupiter is a massive planet used for the creation of anything and everything imaginable, including the pods and bots, as well as ships like the one Milton handed off to me this morning. Massive ships, too, cigar-shaped and moon-shaped and even planet-sized ships that travel the cosmic superhighways to destinations in the universe that would boggle the human mind and lay it to waste to attempt to contemplate such wonders.

Jupiter itself is a creation of a star (not our star) ...that yellow sun that brightens our days with sunshine didn't create Jupiter. The sun(star) gave life to most of the planets and the matter in this solar system. The Sun spits out planets throughout billions of years, flinging most planets out of the star system and into the darkness of space as most stars in galaxies do. Jupiter ejects moons, spits them out when the time is ripe for birth at the end of the production cycle like customized cars off the assembly line.

Jupiter has rings that come and go throughout the ages and have, in the past, been far more prominent than that of Saturn's rings. Many planets have various densities of rings created by the activities taking place inside each planet. Rings are indications of what is happening with the planet, as is true when females become pregnant and their bellies swell and expand then shrink again after giving birth. Rings are spewed from the planet like eruptions from volcanoes. What emerges are telltale signs of schemes inherent in the planet at any given period, stage, phase, and cycle.

Most of Jupiter's moons end up in the frigid outskirts of the star system, where some breach the membrane and enter deep space. Deep space between star systems is littered with billions of planets and moons where reside far different lifeforms than what exists in sunbaked solar systems.

Comparable to a cotton candy machine, Jupiter's atrocious winds mixed with massive internal and external pressure swirl and combine various types of matter and other cosmic material together. Jupiter twerking and churning cosmic substances into the cosmic fabric that forms into solid rocky unique and quirky configurations of moons and endless other types of cosmic products.

JUPITER

Jupiter absorbs and attracts enormous amounts of solar energy from the sun every second of every day, even though the sun is a huge distance away. Jupiter uses that energy entwined with its own internal heat generated at the core to fuel matter manipulation and transformation for the fabrication of everything, mostly unknown to mankind and existing in the shadow of the sun.

Jupiter made its way to this solar system eons ago when our star system was young. Jupiter was born from a nearby star and flung into the icy interstellar region, where Jupiter absorbed massive amounts of material from the galactic soup bowl over the billions of years of its existence. After filling up with cosmic goodies, Jupiter was placed on a trajectory to this star by superbeings.

The cities around Jupiter are exceptional and populated by numerous types of species of the humanoid variety. Hybrids and other kinds of cosmic beings and creatures, not humanoid in any shape or form, have their own niches in the colossal Jovian upper stratosphere.

Some city structures floating in and among the Jovian clouds are cosmopolitan, lively, and open to all with the means, ability, and criteria to enter the cities. Cities are enclosed in structures that deflect pressures and plasma streams generated by powerful magnetic curtains that would annihilate human-classed architecture, space cities, and human spacecraft.

Some Jovian cities are unadulterated, untainted, restricted, cutoff, and off-limits to all, but the inhabitants selected to live in the cities. Undiluted cities provide housing to purebred beings isolated from other species to keep them from cross-pollinating (mentally and physically) and altering the genetic material and structure. Thousands of such purebred cities exist in this region and took up a large portion of Jupiter's airspace far above the planet.

Hybrids are free to enter most cities, even the untainted cities, because Hybrids are sterile, can't breed, and are gene stabilized once activated and turned loose into the utopian colony.

Hybrids don't propagate ideas and concepts with those they encounter. Hybrids do not congregate much, prattle, babble, chatter, prognosticate, indoctrinate, propagandize, or share opinions, views, or feelings. Hybrids have no opinions, no points of view, no ideas, no solutions, no agendas, they simply exist in unadulterated ecstasy.

Hybrids exist for pleasure in a reality where every detail has been figured out for them, and every desire fulfilled for as long as the Hybrids live in utopia. That's the only choice Hybrids make, how long they wish to remain in this or other utopias. Hybrids are free to move to numerous other utopian colonies on any number of star systems in this or other galaxies.

All the cities, cosmopolitan, pure, and everything in between that resided in the utopian colony are utopian grade cities and exist in highly technological realities with copious captivations for entertainment purposes. Utopian cities catered to and supported sophisticated societies with freedom of travel by most occupants via personal ships (pods) within the utopian clusters.

Leaving the utopian clusters happened when members choose to move up to other star systems that are physical or spiritual places with dimensions of their choosing that offered additional soul advancement and development for those bored with utopian life. All members could do so (leave) at any time they wished, they simply up and left after turning in their Hybrid or humanoid bodies and upgraded to newer and far superior models available to them.

This utopia colony is mid-range, a stepping stone and only a temporary place that give the inhabitants a small taste of the things that are available in the billions of stars in the galaxy and the billions of galaxies in the universe where exist colossal and infinite types of adventures and stupendous mind and soul-expanding realities.

My pod entered one of the Jovian cities and easily passed through its extensively fortified defenses without warnings, challenges, or attacks.

"Unauthorized vehicles of the human variety or from other planets and moons with advanced technological capabilities are incinerated, destroyed, blown to bits, often without warning." Declared the Gnokki.

Gnokki was part of my loosely organized and not regimented detail of spirits, spooks, ghouls, and other assorted critters in my cosmic platoon.

Soon after landing, the pod burped me out, shrank, folded itself, and parked inside my handbag. I existed in a cartoon world! The pod did it on its own without instruction from me and would only emerge from the handbag when it sensed I required further use of it. I wished that the Gnokki and their troop of paranormal travelers were that way, park themselves in the handbag and remain serene and inconspicuous more than they were.

"This city has 500 million humanoid residents at any given time, as Hybrid and other types of people came and constantly went to other cities in the colony like at a wine tasting; to get a taste and a feel while sightseeing and sampling unique foods, architecture, and traditions of each exclusive and fantastical city." Clarified, the Gnokki.

The city, a rainforest that I landed in was void of skyscrapers, roads, bridges, factories, office buildings, hospitals, schools, phones, televisions, computers, internet, and electronics of any kind.

The city was a jungle, a literal rainforest with monkeys, apes, lions, tigers, and bears, to name a few of the thousands of animal species and creatures that inhabited the rainforest. It was a spectacular rainforest of tremendous size, scope, and breadth, covering hundreds of square miles of magnificent lush green forest as far as the eyes could see and the mind imagine.

No sign of humanoid life jumped out at me, or did I see when I first arrived in the rainforest. No one there to greet me and my brigade of cosmic critters. I had the key to the city (rainforest) and was free to travel in my pod or walk or glide the endless winding wooded trails that divvied up the rainforest like a million-piece puzzle.

The meat-eater animals roaming around utopian cities and forest cities are not real meat-eaters or plant-eaters. They are life-like synthetic creatures, well-crafted robots, and did not reproduce or stalk animals and Hybrids. No one could tell the difference between the synthetic animals and the real ones other than they didn't attack and eat you when stumbled upon. The vicious-looking animals, lions, tigers, bears, crocodiles, and boa constrictors, and all the rest, are gentle, timid, and friendly but never intrusive.

The forest is a wonderland of tropical wildlife that covered the trees with delightful creatures of every conceivable color in the rainbow, that produced a chorus of pleasing sounds that reverberated all around you. Trees are like large Christmas trees decorated with marvelous ornaments of "real" birds, lizards, squirrels, monkeys, frogs, owls, koalas, chameleons, woodpeckers, snakes, and large scary spiders. Such are only a few of the Earth type creatures in the rainforest, and several varieties not found on Earth roamed the forest too.

"People (Hybrids) lived in huts built on the ground and up in the many layers of the forest canopies to the tippy tops, inside treehouses that bots constructed for the Hybrids. Hybrids coming into the rainforest for the first time moved into one of the many preexisting available huts and treehouses. Huts and treehouses that were left behind by previous inhabitants that vacated for bigger or better huts or had new treehouses built for them or moved permanently out of the forest. Finding empty habitats is easy and convenient. Vacancies are plentiful throughout the jungle without waiting periods." Explained the Gnokki.

Hybrids traveled in pods like the one I have in my handbag (pouch) and had other types of flying devices like the sandals that ferried me around the forests and the cities when I chose not to walk but glide. Walking and hiking are how I enjoyed the outdoors, but the hovering and gliding sandals created extra dimensions to trekking through the endless miles of lush woodland.

Pods accommodated more than one person and up to 2 or 3 people the size of me, roughly 5' 8" and 180 pounds.

Pods are oval, round, squares, spiked, and various other shapes and sizes too bizarre and difficult to describe. Pods are custom made for each Hybrid by servant bots based on Hybrid awareness levels and specifications engrained into each Hybrid during rearing.

Servant-bots fixed all problems in utopia. The extremely few problems that existed in each Hybrid's life and that sprang up within the utopian colony received immediate attention. Bots are an extraordinary and highly efficient autonomous maintenance team that never needed calling or notifying. Bots are equipped with incredible instincts and showed up when things required repairs or modifications promptly.

Pods are colorful, rugged, and rubbery inside and out. Pods are equipped with numerous accessories that materialized into reality with a touch on a floating display screen or from a mental thought projected and captured by that same display screen from the mind. Pods had no propulsion system or guidance mechanisms or control panels other than the display and operated primarily through brain waves of the occupants. Pods take passengers to wherever they had the mind to go. Pods can penetrate barriers, obstacles, and walls regardless of material makeup of barriers except for forbidden places.

Inside each pod is a pleasant, comfortable, and roomy atmosphere even though the pods are not physically large in appearance from the outside. Pods are limited to traveling within the utopian zone and cannot function properly if at all in deep space outside of the utopian zone unless allowed by higher beings, who had abilities to make all things possible.

Pods are universal and can operate under many conditions, including battles when employed on lower planets like Mars, Earth, and Venus, like the one below in the illustration from a painting on Earth.

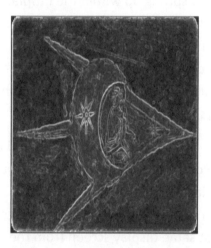

Pods took the form and likeness of the occupant(s) as in Matryoshka nesting dolls. Pods normally had one occupant, and therefore that occupant is prominently displayed on the outer skin of the pod or behind an invisible shield, glass-type enclosure. When more than one person occupied the pod, images of each person appeared on the outer skin of the pod unless the occupant or occupants overrode the system and kept themselves hidden, private from outside view. The Gnokki inside my handbag did not register as being in the pod with me, neither did all the other weird miscellaneous creatures around me and on me due to the nymph exemption.

The handbag shielded and protected everything that was inside of it from everything outside of it. "The control remained with the Gnokki and the other mysterious sprites." I was told by the Gnokki. In other words, the Gnokki could communicate through the handbag with whomever they wished and use the handbag to shield themselves from whomever they decided to hide from. The other critters that didn't join the Gnokki inside the handbag and remained with me inside the pod did not show up on the pod's outer skin; they were excused from exposure and detection.

Looking inside of the handbag and into the medley of the unnatural could make a sane person insane quickly. That explained the craziness of the Gnokki, or perhaps cleverness of the Gnokki. Gnokki made themselves at home in the handbag like genies in a bottle and broadcasted extrasensory soliloquy from there to me and to others and to the Hybrids.

Gnokki didn't emerge from the pouch during my time in the pod, and I don't know for sure if the pod showcased the four-headed Gnokki by displaying them. Gnokki identity could not be exposed by the pod, the handbag, or anything else except by the Gnokki themselves.

The Gnokki disclosed a fraction of their extraordinary selves and abilities...firmly opposed to letting out much about themselves. When Gnokki wanted me to know something impromptu, they unequivocally told me in plain English. An unnerving experience equal to talking to gibbering insects.

Much of what Gnokki incessantly broadcasted, I knew from past experiences and from what Milton shared with me in previous encounters. However, the Gnokki managed to shine a light on information Milton held back on or hesitated to give me. Gnokki were porous and oozed and flung information around like monkeys at the zoo tossing poop at visitors. Much of it about my assignment, even critiquing me and my inferior human-instilled methods. I couldn't absorb material fast enough and retain it, the parts that interested me most, due to the enormous quantity of data blasted at me metaphorically from a sawed-off shotgun by the Gnokki.

The main means of transportation available to the inhabitants of utopia is the type of ships I had available to me, like the ship Milton lent me that morning. The ships (UFOs) are mostly used to transport inhabitants of utopian colonies to the various cities within the colonies or away from the colonies to transfer points for those souls moving higher up the plane of existence and transcending to cosmic places and realities elsewhere.

DOPPELGANGER

The four Gnokki that remained at my house to watch over things during my absence divulged mysterious aspects of themselves while I was on duty in the utopian colony. I discovered at every turn that the Gnokki had tricks up their sleeves that I could never have suspected or imagined. I was notified by one of the Gnokki hanging with me in the land of utopia that my wife, Debbie woke up and went downstairs to my office earlier than usual that morning after I was taken onto Milton's ship. The Gnokki with me was in constant contact with the Gnokki that remained at my house. The Gnokki had made themselves at home in my home and were in the process of fixing themselves breakfast with whatever food they could scrounge from my refrigerator and pantry.

Debbie got up to pee, as normal about that hour of the morning, approximately 2:20 AM, but then decided to ask me something and deviated from going back to bed after her pee and instead walked down to my office looking for me.

My house is a two-story with bedrooms on the second floor and my office situated on the first floor adjacent to the dining room off the kitchen. The Gnokki garrisoned at my house were about to chloroform Debbie and put her back in bed, standard operating procedure, I was told by the Gnokki. The Gnokki uncharacteristically changed plans and decided to implement plan B.

Debbie was in my office wondering where I was and called out my name a few times...and mysteriously, I walked into my office after passing through the dining room from the kitchen, where the Gnokki were hanging out. The four Gnokki had merged into one ME. An exact copy of me. Gnokki became my doppelgänger, a perfect clone of my body and mind but without my soul. I was able to see and hear the whole thing going on in my house as if I was there in the office with Debbie in person. I could see, talk, and interact through the doppelganger as if I was the doppelganger standing in my office with her at that very instant!

Debbie said to my doppelganger that she heard noises and wasn't sure if the noise came from me, totally unaware that she was talking to a mysterious creation fabricated by Alien creatures having breakfast in her kitchen. Debbie said she was worried about me, that I was up late, again, and begged that I go to bed and get some sleep. It was the usual anxiety with Debbie and a typical conversation we've had many times in the past. Debbie couldn't grasp that I didn't sleep much, it baffled her. Debbie sleeps eight to ten hours a night minimum to my 2-4 hours of sleep maximum. Debbie goes to bed early and wakes up late, and I am out and about engaged in some activity when she goes to bed and when she wakes up in the morning.

I assured Debbie through the mouth of the doppelganger that I didn't need much sleep, but for the sake of argument, I was going to bed now, and we walked the flight of stairs up to the bedrooms, together. We kissed, and she entered her bedroom, and my doppelganger entered my bedroom.

The Gnokki dispersed and headed back to the kitchen to finish what they started before Debbie interrupted them...and devoured whatever they had cooked up in the kitchen before Debbie woke up. I was assured by the head Gnokki that they would replace everything they ate and clean up the mess they made before Debbie woke up that morning. And that's when the Gnokki reminded me that it was them and not me that kissed Debbie good night.

"How did Debbie not get a whiff of the food cooking in the kitchen?" I asked the Gnokki. I was told I wouldn't understand. Then it hit me that the Gnokki kissed my wife. The cosmic weasels set the whole thing up!

Anyway, I was elated to know I could communicate with Debbie as if I were there in person with her considering that I was 600 million miles away in Jupiter's orbit, give or take a million miles. Wonders never cease. I did understand that much.

RAINFOREST

The rainforest is the personification of paradise, a wondrous place, city, community, or what-have-you where inhabitants entwined themselves into anything that they conjure up in their wildest dreams and imaginations about living the forest life.

The rainforest in the utopian colony is a place of true freedom and mesmerizing hypnotic beauty where work was not required other than tending a garden or participating with the bots handing them things or fetching stuff as the bots built or refurbished huts and treehouses throughout the rainforest.

Hybrids didn't have to partake in helping the bots, and most didn't. There was never a shortage of habitats and hundreds, if not thousands of livable and available huts and treehouses in the forest, always ready and waiting for occupants.

Energy requirements of the rainforest city are met by osmosis from planet Jupiter. Each of the thousands of cities in the utopian colony extracted matter and dynamic energy directly from planet Jupiter. Jupiter radiates massive amounts of energy from its inner core and its outer shell of turbulence like a gigantic dynamo and creating enough energy to supply portions of the star system with free power forever.

The rainforest is sealed, airtight, and is a natural ecosystem that sustained itself in perpetuity without any assistance from the Hybrids and people, the inhabitants that occupied the rainforest.

Cities in, above, and under the clouds of Jupiter operated in a similar mode as did the rainforest city. Not all the forest cities are rainforest paradises as this one. Many varieties of forested cities are part of the cluster of cities belonging to the utopian colony.

Individual cities had unique types of archaic and futuristic structures and architecture, and everything in-between with divergent utopian systems of operation and entertainment venues to tickle the fantasies of the inhabitants. Sometimes, and under certain conditions and stipulations, visitors too could indulge in innermost fantasies.

The inhabitants of the utopian colony are exclusively adults. No children live in the utopia colony, and no babies can be created by the impotent, barren, infertile-by-design, adult Hybrids, and the other humanoid inhabitants.

Sickness, injuries, aging, or death didn't inflict the people residing in utopia. People (Hybrids) came to utopia fully formed Hybrid adults at the equivalent earth-age of 18 to 35 and remained at the age they arrived for the duration of their residency unless they had a deviated program that specified otherwise.

Hybrids are not tested for integrity and goodness, as humans are on Earth-type planets are. There is no right or wrong, and everyone is gene-perfect concerning physical bodies and mental status and engineered with superb attitudes and friendly behavior. Hate, envy, and violence are impossible in the utopian colonies.

Male and female and everything between existed concerning sexual activity, orientation, and desires. Taboos and perversion have no validity and are nonissues in utopia. Members of utopia don't wed or form bonds or relationships with other members and did whatever they wished to do without restraints.

Soul Mates are not a vital part of this utopic community, nor are other fetishes, complexities, hang-ups and, delusions. But members could rejuvenate and bring to life "segments" of past life experiences that included extracurricular affairs and other encounters with past spouses, friends, relatives, brothers, sisters, mothers, fathers, aunts, uncles, and soul mates, to indulge with and relive special specific memories and moments from any number of past lives not on the prohibited list.

Rainforest Hybrids lived alone mostly, in their own hut by one of the thousands of babbling brooks or in one of the millions of treehouses scattered throughout various levels of the forest canopies. Domiciles are one unit living spaces like single-family homes and "scattered" with a distance from other single units. Clusters of units like apartment complexes or nearby units didn't exist in the rainforest city. No neighbors.

Treehouses are inconspicuous and well camouflaged and hardly visible from the forest floor or from treetops. Structures blended into the natural scenery perfectly having been constructed with living plants and materials harvested from the forest and crafted to be surreptitious by the adroit maintenance bots. Standing directing in front of such stealth structures, most observers would never see the hidden habitats.

Some Hybrids chose to live underground in caves and in tunnels as personal preferences often dictated by deep-rooted desires acquired in previous lives, as all desires are, and allowed to indulge in below ground fantasies.

Hybrids pooped and urinated as did the forest animals, freely wherever and whenever they had the urge without the least bit of hesitation and modesty impeding them. Hybrids are literally forest creatures with animals, insects, and aquatic life. Holding it in could not happen even if they wanted to, while in the rainforest environment. Everything is biodegradable and dissolved back into the ground feeding the roots of the trees, plants, and bushes that produced the food from which the people and animals fed.

For the most part, but not exclusively, animals and creatures are herbivores, as are the Hybrid humanoids. But hybrids love diversification in food choices and enjoyed a wide selection of culinary delights far beyond vegetation.

Hybrids are prolific eaters and mostly consumed vegetation, fruits, berries, nuts, insects, and small critters, easy to pick and easy to catch in the forest. A far cry from the assortment of foods available in the cities where galaxy renowned android chefs created mouthwatering dishes in seconds for the Hybrids.

Hybrids ate everything made available to them from nearby star systems and planets. Land creatures, flying, and aquatic animals from numerous planets that had far different but some similar to Earth creatures too. Lions, bears, sharks, jellyfish, snakes, skunks, wolves, alligators, elephants, etc. Endless thousands of species ended up on the menu as favorite Hybrid dishes.

What surprised me most and left me baffled about the Hybrid menu was a delicacy from the reptilian family of beasts, a species of humanoid shapeshifting, human plaguing "Aliens." Hybrids loved them roasted, toasted, boiled, sautéed, and skewered. However, the downright craziest shit I learned or remembered today; Hybrids also eat humans.

Which prompted me to ask Milton, "Seriously, Milton? Humans are a delicacy here in the land of UTOPIA?"

"Only the bad humans, Michael. Besides, without a soul to flavor the meat, human meat is tough and tasteless, but Hybrids eat it anyway." Replied Milton.

"Do You eat human meat, Milton?" I asked. "Hell no! Michael. No wine in this part of the galaxy goes with 'human carcass,' as some wines do with various kinds of meat, poultry, and fish, Michael."

"Will I end up Hybrid scat working around Hybrid cannibals today, Milton?"

Milton assured me that my garb from his ship protected me from hungry Hybrids, and said that the Hybrids are not cannibals, "Hybrids are not humans," said Milton.

Milton clarified that Hybrids don't kill anything except insects and small critters while foraging in the forests. "Other than that, Hybrids are harmless, sweet, and loving." Insisted Milton.

Unless living in the rainforest as many Hybrids do, food is prepared by bots and androids and ready to eat. Hybrids only see the finished scrumptious product, not the gory mess in the kitchens.

The temperature in the rainforest is a consistent 75-80 degrees, depending on the altitude one was inside the rainforest. High up in the trees and hills, the temperature was cooler than that of the forest floor. Clothing was not an option. Everyone is nude, and Hybrid bodies tolerated the forest temperatures during wake and sleep cycles.

Unlike on Earth, the sleep cycles in the rainforest are based on each Hybrid's desires and not the position of planets, moons, and stars.

The distant sun's effects are negligible on the relatively small footprints of the utopia cities, compared to the size of Jupiter from where the utopia colony's power originates.

Sleep is not a physiological or mental requirement for Hybrids, and no one had to sleep at all if they chose not to. Night and day intervals didn't exist, and people slept or laid around as they saw fit. "Dolce far niente" was the mantra in utopia.

Hybrids had the energy to burn and busied themselves, enjoying primitive life without the primeval hassles of being primitive. Discovering and enjoying the abundance of varieties of fruits and vegetables is a favorite pastime that never ceased to amuse the Hybrids.

New types of sweet and tart fruit surprisingly without warning sprang from vegetation, creating one of a kind rare pleasures enjoyed once in a lifetime for those fortunate to stumble upon them.

Fruit-bearing plants had minds of their own and served to please the Hybrids and astonish and surprise the humanoids with unique food choices. Fruits and vegetables are never out of season, and always available and ripe for harvesting and eating. Cooking over a campfire for those who wished to cook vegetables, fruits, insects, and any number of other delectable things is part of the idealistic lifestyle in the Utopian Colony.

Hybrids bathed in the lakes, streams, and rivers, swam in them, and boated in handmade wooden canoes constructed by the bots, and are found lying around where they would be used by the hybrids.

Theft is impossible and never happened, for there is no reason to steal in the land of abundance with plenty of everything for everyone and never a shortage, want or need. Thieving souls could never enter utopia in the first place.

Sunlight didn't penetrate the rainforest canopy, but light radiated down from the artificially crafted sky, which sustained the plant and animal life as if there were a sun in the sky. The forest city had a glass dome with views of Jupiter and many of its moons that could be seen from the forest floor through the gaps in the trees. Light also radiated up from the forest floor and sustained flower and plant growth under the shade of the multi-layered tree coverings. Internal grow lights generated a profusion of delicate, colorful carpets of flora, forming a magical wonderland inside the deeply rich textured and enchanted multi-level jungle.

The rainforest is music in motions from the sounds of songbirds chirping to the chorus of insects like crickets and cicadas creaking for mates, to the bullfrogs and toads squatting on water lilies croaking under the shadows of low-lying branches in calm waters in multiple forest creeks and magical, illuminated ponds.

TWO SOULS IN ONE HYBRID

Hybrids generally have one soul per body as do most humans, but that depends where they reside. Hybrids located in this utopic colony had extra upgrades available to them not available to Hybrids in other places in the star system.

A specified time after Hybrids are activated with an original soul, Gnokki inserts into the Hybrids an additional companion soul-impersonator from a past life that mimics an old lover, a soul mate situation, or whoever the Hybrid wished to have with them. An extra soul placed inside of their head for as long as they wanted, a memory of that special soul, but not the soul, a kind of recording with a mind of its own to converse with.

Hybrids with soul-partners are never alone and have exciting conversations, including sexual experiences whenever and wherever... they are always a twosome if not a threesome or foursome. The two or more of them spend time at fancy restaurants enjoying concerts and movies together with endless other types of popular activities that couples and friends do together.

Hybrids have fabulous seductive, sensuous times while enjoying scrumptious meals made especially for the two or more of them residing inside one body ("table for one, please") with an appetite for a quartet.

Two doubled soul Hybrids could engage in a foursome and so on. Hybrids giggling to themselves is a normal behavior in the utopian colony as they share intimated feelings and secret desires with each other. Souls and companion souls inside Hybrids never argue, cannot disagree (by design), and get along splendidly. Hybrids could choose to disengage with partner-souls or change partner-souls whenever they wanted.

Gnokki removed soul partners without delay when requested for any reason. Hybrids can turn off a soul partner at any time and for as long as they wished with simple mental commands. Few Hybrids removed partners permanently, according to the Gnokki, but changes in partners happened. More than one soul partner is permitted, and some Hybrids had parties in their heads for extended periods. A crowded mind was not widely popular, but a feature available to Hybrids pushing the edge of sanity.

Hybrid bodies are virtually indestructible and pain-free. Hybrids are like superman without anyone to save, not even themselves. Reckless, egotistical, and stupid is not a Hybrid trait but did happen. Showing off and competing with other Hybrids is very rare.

Hybrids can't improve on perfection, and near-perfect is what Hybrids are. Hybrids are created flawless and exist at levels unattainable by ordinary beings as humans on Earth. Ego-trips are for other peoples in other places and planets in the universe, mostly Earth-type planets, and have no redeeming value in utopia.

Matter exists for souls not quite ready for weaning away from the illusional physical pleasures existing on the physical platforms known as stars and their mirages of planets and moons.

MEAT ILLUSION

Hybrids had flying magical pods of their own for getting around while in the rainforest and could also use pods to leave the rainforest and venture to other exotic places on some of the moons and numerous other cities floating inside or around Jupiter.

Hybrids living in the rainforest could dress up and dine at swank eateries on the five-hundredth floor of one of the thousands of skyscrapers in any one of the neighboring cities/towns and indulge in taboo foods not available in the rainforest city.

Exotic tasty morsels included the availability of every kind of food imaginable along with the standard food selection available on Earth in the meat and seafood department. Real meat, fish, or manufactured meat and aquatic food and anything else Hybrids desired or craved are available throughout the galaxy and in the utopian colony.

Animal protein is created from vegetation via animals and machinery, and both types are available for consumption. Vegetation is made of atoms, and atoms are made from cosmic matter. "Matter" is a void with trinkets of magic held together by webs of figments of imagination. Such trinkets are known to humans as subatomic particles, atoms, protons, electrons, neutrons, with further reductions to elementary particles, quarks, leptons, bosons, and their antimatter cousins.

Atoms are quantum mechanical illusions from the perspective of the 3D mind but contain powerful energy within. The quantum zone is a literal midfield of islands of enormous hidden force in the blackness of space.

In the scheme of everything, astronomical meat and vegetation are mere pixie dust (for lack of a 3D word equivalent), and pixie dust has more substance (energy) in it than all the matter that makes up the whole of the physical universe.

Physical matter is the trickery of the 3D mind created by higher spirit beings existing in the spirit realms for the enjoyment and enslavement of subordinate souls found mostly in the human domains. Human souls are confined inside of physical bodies made of matter, made of nothing but pure mind-boggling energy.

Energy is the rudimentary abilities of higher beings' imaginative cosmic powers to create the illusion of life in the physical minds of humans. Matter exists for souls not quite ready for weaning away from the illusional physical pleasures existing on the physical cosmic platforms known as stars and their mirages of planets and moons.

Everything in utopia is gratis, including for humans like me who don't belong to the utopian society (nonresidents), but labor in the utopian zone for short spells. Full-time humanoid laborers, numbering in the thousands, have chosen their field of endeavor having graduated into the Cosmos.

Synthetic and biological worker bees are cogs propelling vast machinery behind the cosmic curtains and keeping everything moving smoothly.

Towns and cities in the utopia colony are built, maintained, and operated mostly by machines and other types of roaming bot-type creatures that draw energy and function wirelessly from power distribution centers located throughout the utopian cities. Fleshy humanoid types feed at the same places that Hybrids eat, restaurants, cafeterias, and from the vegetation growing in cities and forests.

Hybrids have no need for money, structure, credit/debit cards, keys, phones, computers, identification papers, or officialdom (bureaucracy) to dampen the perfect existence in utopia. Hybrids are free from religion, government dogma, and corporate paradigms that entangled humans on low-level planets like Earth. Hybrids have real and lasting freedom from manmade and natural aggravations and hazards for their entire existence while members of utopic society.

Humans, humanoids, Hybrids, and various other Alien-type beings living in the utopia zone travel to various establishments (cities) in rapid, frenzied motion via ships and other types of flying machines. In comparison, Earth humans' function at the speed of statues due to the limited technology available to Earth humans.

Body waste elimination, purging, is under the full control of the Hybrids the moment they depart the rainforest. Hybrids easily adapted to the changing environments when they visited cities that required a minimum of decorum than living in the jungle al natural amongst the animals, did. Living in modern exotic cities was a far cry from the loose and easy-going lifestyle of romping with the beasts in the wilds of nature, where bowel movements had little need of control, as evidenced in natural settings.

In modern utopian cities, apartments, homes, and public places, toilets are in every room and locations in the cities to accommodate bodily functions and "other" desires. Plant-based toilets turn excrement into compost, which keeps the biological toilets alive and exchanges poop and urine for a flowery fragrance. Scented soft flower parts, petals, stigma, filaments, and pollen tubes work together to leave a clean and dry bottom.

Commodes are actual flowers, large tulips, roses, peonies, and other types of flowers that Hybrids sit on and do their business in comfort, and in full view of other Hybrids in the vicinity. Commodes are a combination toilet, bidet, and spa where private parts get massaged while Hybrids pooped.

Going to the "flower" is exhilarating. Hybrids ate all the time; therefore, squatting on the flower is prevalent in utopia. Sex, pooping, and peeing had zero taboo factors in the midrange physical utopia zones where nudity is the norm and way of life.

CHAPTER 5

DEATH AND HYBRIDS

I headed to my next assignment on moon 3897, a staging area where souls arrived after death, primarily from Earth, but from other planets and moons in the star system too. After souls completed life reviews taken elsewhere on higher dimensions, some are sent to moon 3897.

I greeted a soul of a woman named Julie, who passed away on Earth several years earlier and who had spent that interim after she died with extended family members from past lives in a spiritual place located in the spirit realms. Like most souls, Julie had hundreds of thousands of family members that wined and dined her (not all at once), giving her the royal treatment as family members tend to do in the afterlife zone. Julie was now ready to start a new existence, a new life on a higher level than she was when last alive on Earth. Julie qualified to start her new reality in a physical body in a utopian existence until she decided to move up to higher places.

Julie had earned that privilege during her last life on Earth after toiling many difficult years working and raising a family on her own after her husband, Ralf, died in a work-related accident. Julie maintained a healthy attitude and managed to do well for herself and her two children, Nick and Georgina, during her life on Earth.

Julie died a few years after her children had grown up and moved out on their own, got married, and started their own families.

Death came immediately to Julie after suffering a massive heart attack while at home in her sleep. Julie was spared from feeling any pain during the attack and died peacefully. Julie then instantly found herself surrounded by family and friends that had passed away before her in a wonderfully serene place that overflowed with love and joy. Death by heart attack was by Julie's request before her birth on Earth and allowed to Julie if she met her goals during that life, which Julie did.

I met with Julie on one of the top floors of a huge complex where thousands of such soul-transactions occurred every second of existence. Julie was inside of a temporary physical humanoid body (not a Hybrid body) issued to her by a Grey being that had delivered her to this utopic zone months prior.

During that "time," Julie sampled the wine (lifestyle) of various utopic cities and celestial situations. Julie was shown many of the cities and unique offerings that she could choose to start her new life.

Julie was escorted by a Grey guide who placed her into her temporary body and entertained her the whole time during her visits to hundreds of utopic towns and the realities available to residents.

After the tour ended, the Grey introduced Julie to me, handed her over, and left to fetch another soul from the queue of souls eager for a taste of the utopic lifestyle.

I led Julie into one of the many restaurants and found us a table next to a large window offering spectacular views of the happenings in the immense space outside the glass enclosure with planet Jupiter in the background.

The restaurant itself was equally stunning with fabulous flowing plants draping down from a ledge 100-feet-high near the canopied and multi-layered ceiling. Tropical plants bursting with colorful, fragrant blooms and growing profusely from massive smartly designed gargoyle shaped planters, created a magical adventure in our short promenade through the eatery. Hundreds of people in Julie's situation with their own "Alien" hosts were in the restaurant. Intimate privacy is maintained by the profusion of florae in a jungle setting of extraordinary hues and sweet aromas.

Julie and I sat down at a meticulously dressed out table with satin and lace bordering around a flat diamond-impregnated glass surface. The table sparkled with hundreds of precision-cut facets, each reflecting precious past-life moments and memories belonging to the souls sitting at each table.

The dazzling display of past lives is distracting and disorienting at first, but moods quickly changed, and happy emotions triggered by blissful memories followed with joyful tears. Each person viewed their own memories and not the memories of the others at the table.

The table was decorated with napkins in the shape of doves that took flight soon after sitting and graciously flutter above our heads where they could easily be reached when needed. Fresh, living fragrant flowers folded into the shape of chairs is like sitting on clouds; chairs, park benches, and most seating arrangements in the utopian colony are actual flowers.

Sparkling forks, knives, spoons, candles, and dinnerware added flair and elegance to the table and ambiance for the dinners. One might think it overdone and overwhelming, yet it was a small sample of the lifestyle awaiting souls moving to the utopian colony.

The bistro is one of the thousands of luxurious eating establishments scattered around the utopian colony for Hybrids and others to banquet whenever desired.

Julie and I ordered drinks and appetizers off the menu, which is embedded in the glass top, by tapping on the image of the items we wished to receive. Favorite foods from past lives and realities appeared on the facets of the diamond-encrusted table as optional food choices. Drinks and appetizers appeared instantly up from under the diamond surface.

Engrossed in stupendous amazement by the surroundings, Julie and I munched on appetizers, a selection of roasted sweet mushrooms grown on Jupiter. I sipped on my hot coffee, and Julie drank her iced tea. We talked briefly about her recent past life and other past lives and a few things about what she expected in her future life, the one she was about to begin as a hybrid.

Soothing background music orchestrated by humanoids strumming the strings of marvelously crafted harps and violins vibrated the air with a comforting melody. "The magical instruments from where came the music were made from hardwoods harvested on moon 891," Chimed the Gnokki.

Julie and I communicated in an ancient and gentle language with a wonderful tone like that of angels singing in a choir. A universal language that was not available to human-type beings on Earth-like planets but was readily available to anyone in the utopian region to croon if they so desired. It is a language spoken by the gods and the helpers who could use it during duty/business hours with clients and nowhere else. It's derived from an olden tongue that exists universally inside most souls but remains dormant during physical life on low awareness planets.

I would never use such godly vernacular anywhere other than in utopia. Human ears can't pick up its angelic charms and delicate frequencies, and only hear a squawking, geeky, scratching noise that would drive humans insane had they to endure it for any length of time.

The angelic language is designed to confuse and upset humans, instill fear, using reverse psychology, as "fear not" while undergoing abductions or when in contact with elevated beings.

Julie and I enjoyed a lengthy, slow-paced full course meal from one of our past lives that showed up on the diamond display as food suggestions. All the while, we marveled at magnificent panoramas of planet Jupiter glistening through the dark sky in front of us.

From our perch near the top of the building and a table up against sky-high windows, we observed futuristic (for humans) flying ships rocketing through space, coming and going to moons, and other places of interest of the inhabitants. Flurries of ships and pods involved in loads of activities that would astound humans back on Earth had they a chance to see and know about such cosmic marvels. A dozen Jovian moons were clearly in our view, and some of the larger space cities sparkling like vibrant diamonds off in the distance on the periphery of Jupiter's upper stratosphere. Interplanetary sights never grew old, only more wonderous and mesmerizing each time.

At the end of the meal, Julie and I got up from the table, and I said to Julie, "dinner is on me." Julie laughed, knowing there was no tab, having become an old pro on the benefits of living in Utopia during her time with the Alien guide. The Grey "Alien" showed Julie around various eateries and other entertainment spots in the utopian colony, and she was aware of how things operate before I received her.

"Everything is gratis, what a wonderful feeling to be liberated from survival instinct of having to scrape out a living," Julie quipped excitedly.

"It will take getting used to, now that I'm back in the physical realm as I was when a human on Earth, where nothing is free." Exclaimed Julie.

Everything is "on the house" in the spirit realm where Julie came from having spent time with family and friends the equivalent of five Earth years but a flash in the pan in spirit time. The five Earth years are nothing but a mere trivial slice of time in the back of Julie's memory for the duration of her new life inside a Hybrid body.

Julie and I walked out of the restaurant, which was at full capacity of people in similar situations undergoing similar transactions as Julie and me. Gorging themselves on the marvels of their surroundings and the sensations existing in the overabundant and super-generous universe.

Other types of dealings took place high up in that structured gargantuan cosmic office tower where Hybrids were also preparing for departures away from the utopian colony to higher ground in other star systems and realities available throughout the universe. This place was like a massive train station where spaceships instead of trains brought humanoids into town and took other humanoids out of town to other faraway places in a never-ending procession of cosmic voyages.

The huge complex was mostly offices and hospital type rooms with the upper floors reserved for taking in the cosmic scenery of spectacular Jovian vistas. Various types of restaurants took up the upper floors that served every conceivable food item known in the galaxy, foods that remain unbeknownst to humankind back on Earth until they too make the journey up and out of the human crib, prison, and nuthouse and enter the comic wonderland where mature souls reside for eternity.

I explained the next stage of the process in more detail to Julie following the meal and after the dishes cleared away by robots, and dessert served and enjoyed. I gave Julie the quick rundown of what was to come next. I explained to Julie that she would trade one level of awareness, the one she had now in her temporary container (body) with a higher level of awareness after she was placed into a Hybrid body. The level of awareness Julie had at this moment was more than she had while a human in her last life but not much more. Julie's awareness would increase considerably in the Hybrid body, ten-fold minimum. However, there are tradeoffs, and Julie would lose many memories, considered unneeded baggage and disruptive while living a utopic existence of perpetual bliss.

Every soul in the universe is unique to the core and experienced many lives and situations from different perspectives than other souls, and therefore, there is no uniform awareness concerning human-level souls. Once a soul is placed into a Hybrid container, the awareness levels surge but remain unique to each Hybrid except for the enjoyment bliss aspects, to some degree, remain similar across the board for Hybrids in utopia.

SOUL REMOVAL

I led Julie to one of the surgical rooms inside the massive complex and helped her onto a warm metallic table. Julie then hesitated, looked at me with sad puppy eyes, and asked, "is it going to hurt?" I said, "no," and then I cut her head off. Not really. But sort of.

Julie's soul was removed from her temporary body, and the body was immediately disposed of by the bots. Bots hung out in the surgical rooms and other places throughout the building and looked like ancient Roman sentinels (statues). Part of the furniture, until needed and then became animated, performed assigned duties, and then parked themselves out of sight and out of mind.

Julie's soul, now a crystalize small round spongy object, I placed into my handbag and departed the building having completed that small task, one of many assignments I had that day.

I traveled back to the rainforest city inside my magical flying pod, disembarked, and walked through the enchanted forest for fun, enjoyment and relaxation and to burn off some of that scrumptious food I had eaten. I didn't have a Hybrid body that remained forever fit and trim no matter the quantities of rich foods consumed. I was a human in a human container, and that aspect was not much changed by wearing the "sacred" clothing that gave me invisibility powers and protective shielding from space vermin while leaving my inferior human metabolism intact.

I loved hiking and exploring through jungles and unspoiled natural habitats like the ones found on exotic planets and moons in the utopian zones. And so too did my noisy and nosey Gnokki companions who materialized out of the pouch and shot off in every direction into the rainforest losing themselves in the trees and bushes and gobbling up everything edible they could find.

The Gnokki acted famished and grumbled that they missed out on that fabulous dinner I had with Julie. The Gnokki resented that they could not engage with Julie and others and join us during our meals (Julie was not my first or last soul I dined with that day).

The subsequent removal of Julie's soul from her body after dining with her was a contention with the Gnokki; they wanted to be part of the procedure for some odd reason. I wasn't sure how they were not part of it; they made themselves an ingredient of everything that happened that day. The Gnokki did many things without my knowledge and awareness, and most likely, they had a hand or two in the removal of Judie's soul from her temporary physical shell and kept that information to themselves.

Gnokki understood protocol thoroughly, and they preached it to me every chance they had, which was non-stop all the time. Gnokki supposedly adhered to proper procedure and did not interfere or participate with Julie's beheading, nor spoil the moonlight dinner I had with Julie and the others, whose souls were now inside of my cosmic handbag (pouch).

I would have been ok with the Gnokki doing the dirty work of soul removal, and if they, in fact, did more power to them. It seemed an awful easy procedure removing a soul, and I inclined to credit the feat to the magical garb from my locker.

Inside the handbag exist a strange labyrinthine of nooks, crannies, niches, recesses, holes, small and large spaces, some empty and some filled with profound mystical mystery enough to scorch mind, body, and soul to the level of oblivion. Souls seemingly did fine (ok) inside that maze of cosmic clutter they had to endure and perhaps luxuriate in. It wasn't my job to perform an exit interview, interrogation, or debriefing with each soul after removing them from the handbag to assess their experiences inside the handbag. That was the job of the Gnokki or other such cosmic beings.

No telling where the Gnokki hang out when inside the handbag, but they are hungry when they come out, like ravaging wolves and consume everything in the area. Apparently, no cafeterias or snack machines exist inside the pouch. Souls have their own separate compartments in the labyrinth in the handbag and no way of knowing how many souls are in any one place or even if they communicate with each other while in the bag. When I placed a soul in the pouch, the soul knows where to go, and when I open the bag, the soul next on my list for deployment floats up out of the bag and into my hand.

Similar utopian zones exist throughout the star system that is not of the Hybrid variety and more in line with human life on Earth without the human problems and degradations. They are future habitats for souls moving up the ladder who have graduated from low-level planets like Earth.

Human probes and powerful telescopes can't penetrate or expose utopian zones scattered all over the star system. Human space probes can fly near utopian zones that reside around Jupiter and other planets and moons. But human probes have no abilities to capture more than a passing glimpse, a whiff of the tremendous nonstop mystically cosmic profusion of activity unnoticed and unknown to humans on Earth. Cosmic activity is blocked and hidden by Earth governments and by Alien overlords that don't hesitate to destroy probes, satellites, and ships of violators of cosmic etiquette.

I explored and immensely enjoyed my walks through the woods, discovering bizarre and intriguing insects that showed no fear and never scampered away or flew away when spotted and approached by me and other creatures, including the resident Hybrids.

"The insects are playful and tasteful, like candy that melts in your mouth, and full of nutrients." Added the Gnokki.

Insects are food for the Hybrids and intended to be eaten, like ripe berries off the bush, trees, and plants. Berries of every kind are always in season and readily available throughout the forest in every nook and cranny where a berry bush or tree is producing delectable fruit.

Locating fruits and nuts is as exciting as finding Easter eggs during a hunt as a child. But finding all you could eat in this forest is easy and not a challenge. Nevertheless, discovering unique and exotic fruit and insects is the prize, and Hybrids loved searching for the new stuff that sprung out occasionally, knowing that such delicacies might not be available again for a while or never again.

Figs and dates, two of my favorite fruits on Earth, are far tastier in the utopian rainforest, where all foods are of superb quality.

Nuts (seeds) of every conceivable variety like those found on Earth are a fraction of the exotic foods abundantly available in utopia.

Assortments of edible fungi grew in the shade of underbrush and on the bark of dead trees in the moss-covered forest floor.

A cornucopia of eats is what utopia is all about.

"Shrooms had a sweat aftertaste right out of the ground and off the trees and are ready to consume, and soon to mess with the mind with pleasant dreams and visions created specifically for the consumer of the mysterious and psychedelic produce." Promised the Gnokki.

Mushrooms are colorful and glowed in the shadows of plants, and shimmered and gave off vibrations that are picked up by the brain, a kind of mental handshake to the Hybrids and others who partook of eating the fruit from the enigmatic and boastful forest.

I've seldom enjoyed eating mushrooms nor liked the idea of eating insects, but the mushrooms and insects are mind-boggling tasty and delicious and nothing like the bugs and fungi found on Earth. Insects, small creatures, and vegetables and fruit are not made of the same stuff as Earthly counterparts. Produce in the cities, and the forests are atypical and created exclusively by the gods themselves, who also feasted on the delicacies only available in the utopian zones.

Gods, the true masters of utopian colonies, didn't keep a low profile as they do on Earth and could be seen in plain view hobnobbing with the Hybrids. Gods interacted with Hybrids, ate with them, played games, and mingled openly with inhabitants of utopia. Gods appeared in many physical forms and shapes, often the form and likeness of the inhabitants they mingled with. Everyone knows who the Gods are. Gods didn't hide their true nature and interacted pleasantly with the humanoids and the non-resident helpers. Gods are humble, gracious, loving, and caring, unlike the Gods of Earth that have terrorized humans throughout the ages.

Gods are many, and they came and went their own way from city to city in and around Jupiter and visited the moons and the cities inside of them.

Gods do not reside in utopian colonies; they are transient always on the move roaming throughout the cosmos, galaxy, and universe mindful and attentive of their creations. Gods don't travel in machines and exist in spirit form materializing only when interacting with physical beings. Gods enjoyed drinking and eating with the people, Hybrids, humanoids, and "residuals," a segment of highly mysterious beings, occupying physical and spiritual provinces.

Residual beings are a conundrum and did not mingle with other beings except the Gods. The Gods spent much time with the Residual beings during short stays in the colony.

Hybrids are not curious, inquisitive, or emotional creatures, designed that way and not in awe of the Gods and the mysterious Residual beings who act like sentinels, protectors hiding in the wings throughout the colony.

I got a chance to speak with one of the Gods (superbeings) but only briefly. Gods exist on the same level as Milton, free agents in the universe with absolute autonomy and involved themselves with projects they have interests in. Projects they have created and maintain with an entourage of countless humanoids, androids, robots, spirit, and physical beings. I was one of the small elements (cogs) in the "entourage" working in the fields of the utopian colony and adding my two-cents worth of perspiration to that massive never-ending project.

Washing produce didn't happen and unnecessary, dirt is edible in the forests of utopia. Germs and toxins exist in utopia, as they do everywhere in the cosmos, and served similar biological functions as counterparts on planets and in space, manipulating and tweaking living organic things. Humans have varying tolerances to germs and bacteria, depending on the level of health at any given time. Utopian Hybrids are healthy all the time and foods, and anything natural that entered the mouth is palatable and digestible due to the superior enzymes Hybrids have within them.

Hybrids enjoy cooking and roasting food items in firepits when in the forest environments and on grills in the urban settings of cities as humans do on Earth and, for the same reasons, entice additional flavors to surface for taste buds to explore.

Ready-made baked goods like pies, cakes, and bread are available in the cities produced by servant bots who do most of the food preparations in the cities and forests. Hybrids did the tasting and eating.

Large animals mingled with Hybrids and humanoids without fear of being eaten or humanoids fearful of being eaten by the large animals. Animals are not captured or placed into pens or zoos and roamed freely through the jungle and mixed with humanoids and Hybrids. Animals and insects propagated their own kind as creatures on Earth do. When animals perished, they are recycled back into the ground by the keepers of the city, the bots, that performed the maintenance and requirements of the forests and cities. Flies, maggots and rotting, bloating corpses didn't happen in utopia.

The rainforest is extensive and impossible to get a feel for its grandness and true size without flying over it, and even then, the forest seemingly went on forever. Many trees are huge, old-growth trees, some thousands of years old, others only a few hundred years old. Forest fires never happen, lightning and thunder didn't exist, only gentle rain periodically that kept the plants lush and thriving.

Hiking and exploring the many hidden natural treasures inside caves, caverns, and hollows that spiraled endlessly in every direction underground is an intoxicating treat for those seeking unusual adventures. Interesting subterranean lifeforms unique to each of the hundreds of forests in utopia dazzled with colors and mysterious behaviors when encountered by venturesome explorers.

Aquatic wonderlands, marshes, lakes, streams, babbling brooks and rivers, and countless magnificent waterfalls fed by melting mountain ice, provided cool refreshing clean and great tasting water throughout the forest.

With a population in the millions, the rainforest was, nevertheless, uncrowded and seemed barren of humanoids and Hybrids most of the time I was there. The rainforest is large enough to absorb and conceal most of the Hybrids and animals living in its jungles. Nevertheless, animals are active and often visible, unafraid, and gentle and never a nuisance to the Hybrids. Many of the hominoids did come and go to the other cities in the utopian colony and used the rainforest as a second, third, fourth, or fifth place of residence.

Thousands of unique, encapsulated, enclosed, self-sustaining floating cities above, below and in the clouds of Jupiter, are insignificant in their huge numbers considering that the interior of Jupiter can hold 1500 planets the size of Earth.

Ungodly quantities of cities reside inside of Jupiter's quiet zones, enclaves, unhindered by the chaos that menaces much of the Jovian planet's upper atmosphere. Millions of such cities near the utopian colony are not utopian and are separated and governed by other types of beings, gods, and overlords running things in this solar region. I visited a few of them during this assignment but not entered in my report due to the nature of what the cities harbor and not allowed for disclosure.

The above depiction is a rough simulation of rainforest city when viewed with human eyes. Hybrids have far more visual depth and perception and see more colors and details with higher resolution and clarity than humans. Human perception is skewed by the lack of sunlight and the type of artificial light illuminating the inside of cities and the forests of utopia. Humans perceive a twilight haze where colors blend, and clarity disperse as in a dream.

Hybrid eyes are vivacious with a multicolored glow that, with a single glance, melt human hearts.

HYBRIDS WITHOUT SOULS

Many of the Hybrid humanoids had souls, not all of them did. I was there to insert a soul or two or more into Hybrids without souls. The forest city on moon 3897 is supplied with and received humanoids from various places in the star system and from the first place I traveled to on this assignment, from moon 891. Moon 891 is a major source of Hybrids that populate the rainforest and other cities in the utopia colony. Moon 891 is where Hybrid children are stowed, warehoused, kept and nurtured until needed on other planets, space cities, and moons like this one.

I found the soulless humanoid Hybrids by the signals they emitted from implanted beacons under their skin inserted shortly after their creation and birth on various ET ships. I unite soulless Hybrids with the souls stored in the handbag using a tracking device given to me with other equipment by Milton. Hybrids without souls ran wild and free with other animals in the forest, having more in common with animals than with sentient hybrids and other humanoids. That's what gave the soulless Hybrids away to the humanoid inhabitants with souls.

The humanoids (Hybrids) with souls treated the animals and the soulless humanoids (Hybrids) with kindness as they did with everyone and everything they encountered in the woods and in the cities. Hate and dislike towards anything or anyone at any level at any time had no place in Utopia and did not exist. Utopia is a real paradise with unrivaled harmony for all its inhabitants.

Hybrid humanoids are flesh and blood (well, no blood), as the humans of Earth have. Hybrids have added features but fewer physiological component body parts than humans. Differences are in the genes and types of internal organs or lack thereof. Physical appearance is dissimilar to humans too. Hybrid skin is light-colored and soft, the hair on the head mostly dark. Hybrids are taller than average humans, 6 feet 5 inches was normal for the males and 6 feet for the females. Hybrids are not carbon copies but unique in facial features and physique. Fit and trim are in the genes, which determined everything in Hybrid biological bodies. Hybrid eyes are vivacious with a multicolored glow that, with a single glance, melt human hearts. Those with hearts.

Male and female Hybrids have hair on heads that reached down to the collar and grew no longer than that. Facial hair is nonexistent in the males and the females. Genital hair is less pronounced and nearly invisible compared to that of humans. Hybrids have some hair in the armpits. The rest of the body is hairless, unblemished, and near perfect. Hybrids shed body hair as do humans. Hybrids didn't need to brush their teeth, use soap, shampoo, or deodorant as they produced no plaque, odors, or oily skin. Hybrids don't age, get sick, have bad hair days, become gloomy, or die. Hybrids simply faded away to a higher existence when ready for more fanciful realities than available at the utopian level as this one.

Hybrid humanoids with souls and without souls are naked all the time while in the forest and most of the time when traveling to other cities within the utopian colonies. When not in the nude, skimpy sheer see-through clothing or robes are the attire. Nudity is a natural state of existence on this level of utopia and in all the cities in the utopia federation.

More exotic utopias exist with wide-ranging realities, awareness levels, and freedoms not available at this level utopic region. The higher awareness utopian planets orbit larger stars than this yellow star system and at many more sophisticated levels of spirit functionality with a broader range of dimensions for the inhabitants to expand into.

The old saying, "don't shit where you eat," has never applied in the natural world, the animal kingdom that humans too are part of; the basis and reality of physical existence itself is poop.

I located my first soulless Hybrid humanoid listed on my schedule after hiking three miles deep into the dense rainforest. I chopped my way through with a machete that I found in a box near the entrance from where Milton's ship dropped me off. Crisscrossing trails cleared and easy to traverse without the need for a machete existed, but I chose to explore the undisturbed parts of the forest.

True to the nature of the rainforest, the jungle was thick and lush and closed in around me shortly after slashing my way through the vegetation. I was surprised that I hadn't run into Hybrids or animals, but I could hear animal noises rustling through the bushes as if I was being followed, stalked by wild beasts. Animals are not aggressive or dangerous but noisy, especially the huge numbers and diversity of birds roosting in the trees that squawked like an approaching storm.

The female Hybrid I was searching for didn't have a soul, and therefore had no name assigned to her. The list with information about her that Milton gave me suggested the name Nina, and that's what I called her. I came to a clearing near the river where my instruments showed Nina to be.

Nina was bathing in the river not far from the hut she had claimed and moved into shortly after she was dropped off in the rainforest city along with a few other soulless humanoids, years earlier.

Dropped off by the Greys from a flying saucer, Hybrid humanoids scattered into the forest looking for food like children at a supermarket and running wild through the aisles. Foraging in the cornucopia of delights and feasting off the abundant produce, Hybrids gorged themselves on foodstuffs and the harmony of nature's endless wonders. Humanoids with souls showed more restraint and decorum in eating habits but not much. It didn't matter, obesity and indulging in reckless abandon are gifts from the gods to splurge on while in utopia.

Food guilt is impossible, and so too is getting sick of eating, could not happen. Hybrid metabolism simply processed the food and eliminated the excess, which dropped to the ground and recycled back into the soil. Hybrid poop nourished the plant roots and produced more delicious strawberries, figs, apples, oranges, tomatoes, radishes, peppers, pears, bananas, peaches, cherries, apricots, plums, dates, and an endless assortment of edible delights far too numerous and unique to mention. That's the magic of poop.

Nina was alone in the shallow stream, splashing in the water like a four-year-old child and having a good time. But there was more to Nina's splashing around, she was eating crawdads that she caught by stirring up the water. And as I watched from the shore, Nina then dove into the water again after spotting a frog, caught it, and ate it raw as she had with the crawdads.

The forest was as natural as nature intended (designed that way by the local gods), where animal defecation was a major part of the ecology engine that sustained the natural physical world from top to bottom. The same system as with the aquatic life found in ponds, streams, rivers, lakes, seas, and oceans back on Earth that are toilets, where consumption and defecation go hand in hand with the thousands of aquatic species existing in the aquatic latrine. The old saying, "don't shit where you eat," has never applied to the natural order of things, the animal kingdom that humans are part of. The basis and reality of physical existence itself is crap (poop). Crap is matter and matter is pixie dust, and pixie dust is nothing more than a projection from the higher echelon of superbeings lavishing existence on mortals and immortals alike.

On Earth, the natural order with all its germs and viruses is more complex and more deadly to the delicate human physiology that has since lost most of its immunity during the modern germ-free sterile era.

I contacted Nina by waving at her to come out of the water and onto the land near her hut. After seeing me, she didn't panic and run like some while animal back on Earth but quickly and eagerly came out of the water as if she was glad to see me. Nina walked up to me, dripping wet and stark naked and looked at me curiously like a confused puppy and offered up a friendly smile in my direction.

Nina's eyes are greyish brown, not yet the sparklingly glowing eyes she would have once a soul found its way into her brain. Nina didn't talk, couldn't talk; she lacked experiences and abilities and a soul to put things into perspective. A soul is a basic requirement for her to be able to project out into the physical world, her feelings, thoughts, and desires.

Nina could not communicate intelligently, only able to grunt. The magical cosmic trinkets I carried inside my handbag was lacking inside her mind and brain. Or I should say most of the things the Gnokki harbored within themselves and uploaded tidbits of their cosmic elements into the minds and bodies of the soulless Hybrids like Nina.

I pulled out from my handbag an incapacitated encapsulated dormant soul, matched it with the dripping-wet Hybrid soulless Nina, and pressed the soul into Nina's Hybrid forehead, gently. I performed the delicate procedure after having softened the entry point on her skull with a liquified solution that presented itself soon after the soul jumped from the pouch into my hand. After a moment passed, the wound on Nina's head closed and healed instantly. Nina whimpered for a few seconds and then went and laid down in her hut that we were standing near. I gave Nina a few minutes to rest and adjust to her higher awareness level and waited for her to come out when she was ready.

Huts in the rainforest are nothing like the blood-sucking bug-infested huts in poor countries back on Earth.

Straw huts in utopia are comfortable and equipped with pillows and mattresses made from soft, durable grasses that grow in the fields abundantly, and free of infestation from pesky parasitic insects. "Pesky" didn't exist, but insects did, and Hybrids ate bugs as if they were jellybeans.

Hybrids with souls with the help of bots, fairies, and other forest critters interlaced the grasses into pillows and mattresses and added interesting features and personal touches to drab made-of-straw and bamboo, huts and the straw furniture in the huts. Utensils carved from wood and cooking apparatus for cooking over campfires and hollowed out wood bowls came with the huts.

Bowls and utensils are made for the Hybrids and adorned the hut that Nina moved into it. Food storage was unnecessary and, therefore, didn't take up space in the hut. Huts are small and used to sleep or nap with hardly any other use. Hybrids spent most of their time foraging endlessly in the forests, and swimming and frolicking with other Hybrids and animals in the creeks and lagoons.

Streams, ponds, rivers, and lakes offered additional food choices, fish, octopuses, squid, crabs, oysters, and endless types of aquatic life that Hybrids loved gobbling up. Not all the Hybrids expanded their food choices to include raw aquatic food; it was a personal preference that lingered from habits and desires enjoyed in past primitive lives in other lifetimes. Cooking food over a campfire is another element popular with hybrids when alone or with other Hybrids who happened by to play and engage in erotic activities.

Utopia is void of sports, politics, hobbies, movies, and other mundane things to talk about and occupy mind, body, and soul. Thus, conversations are minimal and play and exploration maximal as it is with children on Earth whose minds are unfettered with needless stuff.

Adult Hybrids are child-like in actions and activities, having no cares, worries, or hang-ups to hinder the enjoyment of life. Hybrids leaned towards solitude, returning to huts and treehouses alone after romping in the woods with other Hybrids and assorted creatures. However, Hybrids are never alone. Those with souls had soul companions or options for additional souls inside of them to banter with.

Hybrids have no time awareness, no night and day division, and are consumed by "individual" activity without conscious awareness of the activities of "others" and their personal events and happenings. Activity (the hustle and bustle) in general remains constant throughout the utopian colony, which is a very busy place when viewed from the outside looking in by non-residents not absorbed and preoccupied with individual pleasure-seeking.

Luminosity (light) in the rainforest and other cities is artificial light that fluctuated and glowed more radiant in some places and shimmering twilight in other places without rhyme or reason and came in like a rolling fog off the ocean. Ethereal translucent otherworldly existence was dream-like, yet awareness was heightened to levels unknown in the human realm. A cerebral sensation far more penetrating into the soul than anything humans on

Earth could grasp or experience while in a human mind and body...a three-dimensional slot.

Occasional spontaneous large gatherings occurred without notice or preparations or reasons where Hybrids congregated like schools of fish or swarms of birds dancing and converging and splitting apart and merging in a sensuous ballet. A spontaneous phenomenon that even the Gnokki failed to explain in a way that made sense to my three-dimensional mind.

My godly and gaudy attire from my locker in Milton's ship worked wonders in my ability to transcend dimensions, but with limits that left me stumped about many mysterious concepts and happenings in the land of utopia. So much of the reality that Hybrids existed in and immensely enjoyed are privileged to the Hybrids alone. Hybrids exist at an awareness level not accessible to worker-bees as me and many other types of auxiliary beings and creatures. We are on the fringes of a cosmic embryo while it squirms inside of an amniotic bubble (utopian colony) as we attempt to fulfill our individual duties. My personal perceptions of utopia were skewed, an outsider's point of view is all I could muster.

Utopian colonies undergo a process that takes them to mature status and then close like clams and travel slowly, migrating through the star system like a fish in the open seas. Sometimes returning to the original place of formation or slipping away to other star systems in the galaxy or beyond.

Hybrids undergo a transition that takes them to higher realms of awareness and existence, a transformation to spiritual places in ever-increasing higher dimensions. Hybrids could choose to withdraw from the process and often did knowing they were not ready, willing, or able to further an astronomical pursuit of no return, in a particular category of existence and reality.

In utopia, an awakening takes Hybrids to places beyond the normal human engagements and bonds that stitch souls to other realities within themselves. Every utopian colony is unique in the aspects of soul manipulation, transformation, and development. In such utopian colonies, family, and friendship attachments fall permanently to the wayside, and vast new realities without the bonds of family and friendship emerge. Such radical thoughts are soul-wrenching for most humans who are entwined with loved ones that they have shared countless lifetimes and infinite memories and are loath to abandon.

In this utopia, mental attachment to and with other Hybrids cannot happen, did not happen, never happened. Hybrids didn't fall in love with other Hybrids or form bonds of any kind. Love for all things is a natural state of reality that is adequate, fulfilling, and part of the DNA contrived psychic software installed into the Hybrid's physical brain and mystical minds.

Sexuality is a spiritual element that binds physical entities with each other in ways that supersede other types of mental attachments and affections while in the physical plane. In the Hybrid colony, sexuality is spontaneous when two or more Hybrids felt the mood, they made it happen or let it happen, and it happened as natural as could be devised by the higher beings, but with no lingering attachments. Sexual acts had no bonding aftereffects on the hybrids as they often do with humans.

Super Beings, the purveyors of utopias orchestrated this level of reality for the Hybrids chosen to experience the unique existence. Utopias and their exclusive populations are not on the same trajectory as other utopias. Each utopic colony procures and creates unique and different paths for members to flourish into like a flower blooming in a garden of thousands of florae with their matchless petals, colors, and fragrances, forever distinct from the rest.

Endless millions of such transient utopian colonies exist in galaxies, and endless billions exist in the universe, blinking in and out of space like twinkling stars in a Vincent van Gogh starry night sky.

Next, to gorging on food, victuals, grub, is gorging on sexual pleasures profusely, as the entire Hybrid reality surpassed the physical and entered the surreal, magical world of the supernatural wonderland. One activity flowed seamlessly to other activities, weaved into patters as diverse as homemade afghans on display at a massive convention hall.

Multiple patterns and erotic designs flowed through the Hybrid minds as hybrids frolicked in the rainforest alone or accompanied in wonderment and amazement at every delectable moment. Afterward, Hybrids retreated to huts or numerous other habitats with or without companions for short naps, followed by soothing swims and more frolicking through the enchanted forest, probing for additional pleasurable events both physical and illusional.

Illusions and delusions and hallucinations are games Hybrids engage in with the forest creatures, the fairies, pixies, elves, goblins, and so many other types of entities existing throughout the woods. Hybrids are saddled with insatiable desires and the energy to pursue relentlessly every fantasy they can conjure.

Remaining in this rainforest city was voluntary, and any of the Hybrid humanoid inhabitants could choose to leave anytime and visit or permanently relocate to anywhere in the utopian zone. Most, but not all the cities in the conglomeration of utopian cities are open to the members of said society.

After a time, Hybrids found other cities in the colony that suited them more than the rainforest city, where most choose to start when first initiated into the utopian colony. Many types of forested cities to pick from for those that preferred living the wildlife on levels of reality and awareness few could dare to imagine.

Hybrids pursued endless hobbies and activities programmed into them by the administrators of the forested cities or the brick and mortar cities they visited or chose to live in. The majority of Hybrids preferred traveling from city to city and place to place and village to village sampling unique cultures, foods, and social delicacies unique to each city. Hybrid members could devote their entire existence in utopian colonies if they had no want for higher realms or lower ones.

Some utopian colonies closed like a flower after blooming and dropped out of sight swallowed into an array of dimensional plasma never to be seen again in the universe of its birth and creation. Hybrids and other members are alerted and allowed passage to supplementary places and other realities before the event to allow for escape. After the event, no additional information about the colony and its inhabitants could be known by anyone other than the Superbeings.

After some time passed, equivalent to ten minutes, Nina emerged from the hut, came up to me, and we talked a little as she was not used to being "alive." Nina was all giggles, happy, excited, and jumping around like a little girl on steroids on the playground during recess. The adjustment to Nina's new awareness was not complicated, nor did it take long because all the pertinent "software" was uploaded into her mind by the Gnokki before I placed her soul into her Hybrid brain. Gnokki would visit Nina again at some point and install a companion soul into her mind when they knew the time was right for that to happen, and if Nina wanted a companion in her head.

Nina calmed down and came up to me and hugged me, and we talked a little more about her new awareness and desires that came with knowing infinitely more than she did moments before her soul was physically implanted into her brain. Abruptly, during our genteel conversation, Nina squatted low to the ground and dropped pellets and urinated. Nina quickly stood back up and said, "oh my," "I would have been mortified, so embarrassed, ashamed had I done that back on Earth."

I responded, "Back on Earth, the natural frightens the hell out of most civilized people." She said it was unexpected, but she was not bothered the least having done it and in the presence of another sentient being, me. I told her that plant life and humanoids, Hybrids, humans, and animals have a symbiotic relationship. Plants create magical delicious, nutritious food for the animals and humanoids to eat, from which comes the fertilizer (food) that plants feast on from the bowels of humanoids and other animals. "A mutually beneficial symbiotic system," I said to Nina.

Nina shrugged, like, "so what." I laughed at her indifferent response, which confirmed that the implanted personality into her mind by the Gnokki was a success.

About then, a butterfly landed on Nina's nose, and that would have made a beautiful picture, had photos not been forbidden in utopia. Nina, without giving it much thought, grabbed the butterfly by the wings and put it in her mouth and ate it.

"Insects are edible and delicious and highly nutritious." The Gnokki chimed in and said to Nina.

Nina agreed and replied, "I would have barfed had a bug got anywhere near my mouth when I was a human on Earth. And now I'm going to go find other delicious bugs to eat!" And Nina dashed off into the forest like a freed antelope and perhaps never to be seen by me again.

The Gnokki followed Nina into the woods, but she remained unaware of them, even though she heard them speak to her moments earlier, perhaps thinking it was me.

One Hybrid checked off my list and several more to go, I told myself, or perhaps it was the Gnokki tossing things into my mind like tossing horseshoes. I was never sure about cosmic rascals and their freakish abilities to manipulate minds, bodies, and surroundings.

Nina had no recollection of her time in utopia prior to me inserting her soul into her Hybrid body. She didn't remember that she ate insects and small animals and lived as a wild animal herself up to this point. Now, Nina is a conscious and fully aware wild animal, more aware than any human on Earth-type planets could ever be or comprehend. Humans who viewed and considered themselves highly civilized and entirely aware of the goings-on in their daily lives and affairs are, in reality, locked into their own delusions...as are the hybrids but on a higher and diverse level.

Frogs, toads, crickets, snakes, snails, lizards, moths, butterflies, walking sticks, slugs, scorpions, birds, and thousands more creepy-crawly and flying creatures similar to creatures found on Earth only added a fraction to the massive numbers of small critters existing in the rainforest. Creatures the Hybrids enjoy observing, interacting with, and munching on.

Edible and incredibly melt-in-your-mouth tasty bugs are organic and without sentient qualities or souls. And like magic mushrooms, several varieties in this forest, the insects, having been consumed, eaten, took the Hybrid minds to marvelous, magical places beyond the rainbow to unique niches of realities that corresponded to realities, experiences and travels that the insect or small animal had witnessed and experienced and transferred those stored experiences to the eater, the Hybrids.

Utopia is a hedonistic paradise, a playground of never-ending comfort and pleasures. Ironically, a paradise reserved for industrious souls and a place where the lazy need not apply... forever stuck on the merry-go-round of reincarnations in futile search of concepts of little merit.

Fantastical insects added magnificent animated color schemes to the landscape, which changed with the sway of the breeze and transformed when the gentle rain misted the magical creatures causing them to light up like fireflies.

Psychedelic, hallucinogenic, mind-altering trips are a huge part of reality in the utopian regions with no harmful side effects or negative experiences like the undesirable effects that contraband on Earth harbors and delivers to humans. In utopia, the mind and body exist on many levels of enchantment, great pleasure, and delightful fun with multiple dimensions to enhance every experience. Unfathomable realities to humanoids living outside the boundaries of utopia.

Everything in the forest is edible. Flowers, grass, plants, trees, bushes, the bark on the trees, the leaves, and even the dirt. Fauna and flora had its own unique flavor and the mind-blowing and altering journey that came with it. Spiders are edible and spun wild dreams (pardon the pun) and tantalizing visions in the minds of those Hybrids who ate spiders.

Toads, lizards, frogs, snakes, scorpions, tarantulas, and any number of small critters are delicacies of cosmic proportions for the Hybrids. Hybrid humanoids had only to touch the insects, small creatures, plants, flowers, or whatever, and they crystallized into a sweet delectable confectionery that was truly dandy for mind, body, and soul, for those with souls.

Hybrids without souls enjoyed everything the Hybrids with souls enjoyed but on different levels of awareness. Similar awareness levels and situations that humans have with pets on Earth. Soulless Hybrids are at the equivalent levels of awareness as many humans with souls.

The whole idea of it gave me a headache. I was a human in a human body, and the robe and sandals couldn't shield me from the bohemian extravagance avalanche run amuck that existed in utopia. It was too much for a mere human immortal to handle.

CHAPTER 6

Sex in a Hybrid utopia is for pleasure only and not for reproductive purposes. Male semen had no sperm value and is a substance with multiple hidden qualities triggered by each individual Hybrid that the semen comes in contact with (every sexual encounter is unique). Female Hybrid bodies are void of eggs and milk glands. The uterus secretes an orgasmic tonic during intercourse that stimulates exclusive experiences for each partner. Female breasts yield a stimulating elixir when aroused.

Female breasts are small and firm, never having to produce baby milk and enlarge for children to suckle, and sag with age. Males have multipurpose penises that clamped on to the female's uterus and anus like fingers, on a third hand, an entirely Alien sensual system compared to human male sexuality.

The whole of the Hybrid existence, mind, and body is pleasure-driven, pleasure-seeking, pleasure arousing, and pleasure for the sake of pleasure.

The whole idea of it gave me a headache. I was a human in a human body, and the robe and sandals couldn't shield me from the bohemian extravagance avalanche run amuck that existed in utopia. It was too much for a mere human immortal to handle.

I wanted it! I needed it, I would sell my soul for it, but only those who merited received it. Nothing evil about the blatant wantonness only attainable in its uncorrupted form in the utopian colonies.

Excessiveness and extravagance didn't harm anyone. Instead, it was a heavenly token given to the residents by the gods (Higher beings ruling over galaxies and star systems that created billions of utopias like this one). Delights enjoyed by gods and angels themselves who graciously rained down such pleasure on the Hybrids like rays of sunshine.

Intemperance (gluttony) is hardwired into Hybrid bodies, minds, and souls before and after a soul is placed into the Hybrids. Hybrids had no choice but to enjoy every morsel of their existence to the nth degree without ever experiencing the seesaws of highs and lows. Only highs do Hybrids experience never-ending highs, good times, and good feelings all the time for as long as they live in the utopian colony.

Contemplating it from a human perspective and ideology gave me another and a bigger headache. Being an Earth human, I existed in a death-grip of contrived human guilt from the simple selfish thoughts of the many wonders I visited during my assignment. Shame and ignorance are constantly and ruthlessly pounded into the human psyche day after day from the very moment of birth on planet Earth until death, by the demons ruling over that sanctimonious blue planet, Earth.

The young woman, Nina that dashed off in search of delightful bugs to eat, had been in the rainforest city the equivalent of 3 years, in animal form without a human class soul and only awakened when her soul was insert into her Hybrid container. Nina foraged and frolicked with others like herself, soulless Hybrids and hybrids with souls, for a long time and remained mostly unaware, unconscious of much of the things sentient beings are aware of.

Now with a soul, Nina has far more dimensions to play with and explore inside her mind. Nina has visual and colorful vistas, and more sexual vitality, and is now pleasure conscious. Nina existed in a blank state of mind, in a black and white world without color perception and operating on bare minimum instincts as wild animals, critters, insects, and like most humans on Earth, do.

On Earth, animals without souls have built into their brains powerful instincts that protect them from danger and helps them find food and shelter, such as maternal instincts of caring for offspring. Instincts are important on lower level planets like Earth but not here in utopia country where survival is a given, a done deal, and not an effort on anyone's part, sentient or not.

HERE TODAY GONE TOMORROW

Utopian colonies are transient colonies. Like bees, they swarmed from planet to planet and from star system to star system even from galaxy to galaxy and often into the dark space between galaxies around rogue planets lost in the cosmic blackness. Utopian colonies can remain in one place for millennia, thousands of years, hundreds of years or a few years, or very short spans of time, even a few Earth days, weeks, months, or seconds.

Utopian colonies magically vanish and reappear in other places in the star system or across the galaxy, or across the universe, instantaneously. Endless millions of such transient utopian colonies exist in galaxies, and endless billions exist in the universe, blinking in and out of space like twinkling stars enfolded in a Vincent Van Gogh Staring Night sky.

Only members of the utopian colonies traveled with the transitioning utopian colonies. Everything not belonging to the utopian colonies, including me and Milton's ship and thousands of other such ships and soulless Hybrids without souls to anchor them to the utopian colony, would be left behind like space junk.

Space junk eventually burns up in the atmosphere of planets or incinerated by stars. Most junk ends up in the outer reaches of star systems as interstellar debris in a cosmic soup of material made up of moons, dwarf planets, asteroids, dust, comets, and ice, called the Oort Cloud and its smaller sister the Kuiper Cloud or Belt, by human cosmologists and astronomists.

A dazzling array of realities exist inside utopian colonies. Literally, thousands of unique cities catered to every wish and desire of the inhabitants. One city I visited and that affected me as if I was one of the inhabitant members triggered a swarm of memories from past lives back into the forefront of my mind. So real were the memories that I was nearly knocked off my focus by a new reality that nearly sidetracked me from my main assignment. Souls and Hybrids required my attention, and I could feel the souls' impatient essence squirming inside my handbag like escargot wanting out of their shells and craving to be joined with their Hybrid bodies.

They would have to wait. After all, I was the one in charge of the handbag and not the squirming souls. Yup, abuse of power it was. Lucky for the disembodied souls, there are plenty of things in the handbag to keep them distracted and amused until unification. The Gnokki critters that came and went and other "things" far more mysterious and permanently residing inside the handbag played host to the souls in the handbag.

Some of my favorite people from several of my previous lives came to life, and I was able to enjoy the sweet moments that we shared so many ages past. These were not illusions or projected fantasies, these were real situations with real souls who were whisked into a dream state on their end of existence, to visit with me in the flesh, in the here and now, today, on my end of existence.

They were somewhat confused until I reminded them, they are in a dream but alive and awake, physical and in-person inside a magical utopian city from where I summoned them. They didn't understand or grasp the meaning of the encounter as they were in a dream "reality" even though they were in physical form and communicating with me in the physical realm. We rejoined pleasant moments in real-time, exactly as it happened originally many moons ago that made us best of friends, associates or lovers.

One such visitor was a girl named Vita, who I had a crush on during our adolescent years that took place on a utopian planet many lightyears from this star system and this galaxy, the Milky Way Galaxy.

We were children on a planet circling a star in a galaxy quite a distance from the Milky Way galaxy. It was a galaxy astronomically and incomprehensibly far from where I am now. Vita laughed when I said, "Milky Way," a galaxy she never heard of and made no sense to her at all. "Is it made of milk?" She joked with a giggle.

I tried to explain to Vita how the name came about, and she laughed again and said, "I don't care, I really don't." At that moment it occurred to me that I was a young boy again, about the age of fifteen and she a young girl of sixteen or seventeen. We lived in a village prosperous and pristine that equated to the early eighteen-hundreds Earth era. It was a utopian village lacking in crime, hate, sickness, war, and famine with all the perks of a paradise but missing modern amenities.

The village could have been located on Earth, the similarities were uncanny, a similar yellow sun brightened the day sky, and a single gleaming moon lit up the night sky. It was a real fairytale existence without the evil cannibalistic witches and conniving wolves that eat children as is told to frighten children here on Earth. No gory fairytales or fairytales at all existed in that village on planet G58.

The village had schools, and shops and people grew up and got married and had children and then grandchildren. It was a normal peaceful life where "everyone" lived happily ever after, for real. Life span was 135 years, and people lived to that ripe old age and then stopped, dropped dead, died, and went somewhere else, to some other planet or came back to planet G58.

Bodies of the dead are cremated, and ashes placed back into the ground, and sorrow unknown and unwarranted, and the departed forgotten until meeting again in the afterlife. People didn't die from accidents or illness, they died when they reached their 135th birthday. People knew when they were going to die, and that was accepted as a natural progression to other lives and realities in the universe.

Unlike on Earth, where most everything is a mystery and an unknown, on planet G58, most things are known and understood by everyone. They didn't have modern conveniences, airplanes, rocket ships, television, internet, phones, and cars, but they knew such things existed on other planets because those things, concepts, are taught in schools. Schools have access to a vast library of knowledge that existed from the planet's inception and upgraded by the "elders" who wrote books about cosmic knowledge given to them by beings from the stars.

Back on Vita's planet, which was also my planet at that time, I owned a horse, she owned a horse, everyone had horses to gallop around the town with. People kept chickens, hogs, ducks, dogs, and cats and raised most of their food on plots of land they owned and farmed. Life was like on planet Earth before the modern age. And I told that to Vita.

Vita's young mind was fascinated that Earth had all the things we had back on our old planet and much more. Earth was a space-age planet, and Vita told me she wanted to live there, on Earth with me. Until I "reminded" Vita about the wars, the hunger, the crime, hate, envy, sickness, and sorrows, and that death haunts constantly and can take you or loved ones at any age at any time.

Hearing that from me, Vita remembered the reality of capricious existence on non-utopian planets and decided she didn't want to live on Earth after all. I asked Vita where she was living now, but she was confused because she was only a memory come back to life with limited access to her soul. Vita believed she was living on planet G58, where we met and grew up as children and from where my "memory" of her originated.

Vita had been to other planets since that time but requested to return to planet G58 but wasn't sure if that's where she was now. Vita loved the village so much she continued requesting to go back to planet G58 and the simple lifestyle, but she did change it up by trying other planets and other time slots.

Vita told me that she had few memories and many gaps between her lives on planet G58, which numbered in the hundreds of years if not thousands of missing years blocked out of her memories.

Vita came back to me now in the utopian city as a female, from the time we shared life on that planet together but was now a he, in her present existence on some other planet and could not say more than that. During the interim, Vita had been many other things and other genders for the thousands of years since we were children in that distant galaxy.

Our lives had intertwined many times and even more recently than I was currently aware of. Vita and I existed on several star systems in the Milky Way Galaxy, the galaxy she made fun of the name.

Galaxies, stars, and planets have different names on other planets from what humans call them. But similar names too. Humans are unaware of most stars in the Milky Way Galaxy and therefore have no names for them. And have no names or knowledge concerning 99.9856...of the galaxies and stars existing in the universe. On Vita's planet, where they live in the horse and buggy era in perpetuity, a period that is locked in place that never changes or modernizes, they know infinitely more than what space-age humans on Earth know about the universe.

I soon realized that summoning Vita was like opening a can of worms, a Pandora's Box. Due to the confusion of mind when contacting past physical beings that carry a collected history of previous lives with the potential to tarnish or taint old memories and future realities.

Vita wanted to make love to me as we had done many times back in the village every single day until we grew up and went our separate ways. I became an apprenticed blacksmith in another village a few miles away, and Vita a teacher in the village we grew up in. I married a woman, the blacksmith's daughter, and had three children with her. Vita never married, choosing to remain single for the duration of that life.

No one on planet G58 married until the age of twenty-two when males and females became fertile and achieved a short window for bearing children. The window lasted five years, and then the adults, males, and females became infertile, unable to produce children ever again.

Under the age of twenty-two, people were free to frolic and cavort openly without worry of becoming pregnant or reputations soiled. Sexuality on planet G58, as is true on most planets, is viewed as a routine bodily function that never raised an eyebrow or a giggle being it was commonplace, and everyone indulged in sex until they died.

Religion didn't exist on planet G58, and neither did governments or other forms of bureaucracy. Each village had a grocery store or two, a butcher shop, a bakery, a cobbler, a schoolhouse, a tinsmith, a foundry, a glassmaker, and a bank and a few other establishments that provided the needs of the people.

Bartering and exchanging things for other things was popular, but coins for currency are also available for transactions and used to buy essentials. Much of the food and goods in the store came from the community of people who had surplus items to sell; eggs, hens, pork, fish and things from the garden, tomatoes, corn, beans, fruits, and canned goods (preserves), to sell or exchange. Other homemade items like clothing and assorted household things are available for purchase or trade at the store.

While in the utopia city during my assignment from Milton, I was literally fifteen years old in body, and Vita sixteen years old in body and "mind." My young hormones were jolted when Vita made her moves on me, but I had no intention of doing anything sexual with her. I was already distracted from my duties as it was.

Vita's memories came on suddenly and evaporated just as suddenly. Vita told me she is nearby, living in a star system a few million lightyears away in the Andromeda galaxy, where she is "something else" and had no other details she could comprehend and narrate to me.

I attempted to put the genie back in the bottle when I realized I was endeavoring to reason with a horny teenage mind from the distant past with psychotic memory issues. Vita's situation was not out of the norm, considering she was a memory from my mind recreated and brought back to life by a supernatural device I subjected myself to while visiting one of the utopian cities.

My mind was protected by the wardrobe from Milton's ship, and it remained intact and did not shrink in chronological age as Vita's mind had to match her chronological age. Nevertheless, Vita was every bit alive in a physical body, and her mind and a shard of her soul were present in the room where my experience with Vita activated and became real.

As in a dream, situations changed from one reality to some other reality for unexplainable reasons that remain beyond human 3D comprehension.

Vita asked me what I had inside my purse (handbag), and I told her nothing important, in hopes of swaying her curiosity to something else. It didn't work, and Vita wanted to see for herself, and so I handed her the handbag. Vita turned it around every which way and could not find the opening. Vita handed the bag back to me, and

I, too, could not find the opening. The handbag closed itself off for the duration of my dereliction of duty.

The encounter with Vita's fractured reality spiraled out of my control, and I bid Vita farewell and managed to stop the transmission that brought her back into my life from a long-ago memory that took place thousands of years in the past. It worked, and I jumped into my pod and left that city of dreams.

I was able to control who I wished to be with at any given time, meaning one soul at a time and not the whole gang from various lifetimes with diverse interests, friendships, and motivations, which I could have chosen. And god forbid I had done that and had to deal with a bunch of past relationships all at once. That reality and ability exist in numerous utopian "dream cities" in the colony, and I made sure not to be tempted, enticed, sucked in as I was with Vita when I visited other seductive cities.

I was limited on how much time I could use for my own personal pleasure and potential demise during business hours and during my existing life on Earth which barred, banned me from lavishing on myself excessive cosmic delicacies, treats and privations too. Members of the utopian colonies would not have incurred the difficulties I experienced because they belonged there, are citizens of utopia, and had leeway, privileges, latitudes, and allowances not available to nonmembers as myself.

NUMEROUS SOULMATES

Humans with multiple marriages, divorces, and relationships have come into their lives on Earth, followed by various interested parties from other lifetimes who consciously intended to hook up with them at some point during that "particular" lifetime. There are no "chance" encounters with the people we meet in life. Souls that are determined to interact with other souls eventually find ways to devise and achieve specific goals with the help of preprogramming before entering a specific life during a reincarnation situation.

Most people, if not all people, are not aware of these hidden destinies, manipulations programmed into their lives before birth, always assuming that everything that happens in life is happenstance, coincidental.

Destiny with a clause is real and can be hacked by conniving souls with the help of cosmic cohorts, is "sometimes" how souls (people) get into other people's lives as children, spouses, friends, enemies, parents, coconspirators, etc. Many successful and failed marriages, business partnerships, and musical band groups form, come together via such divine celestial loopholes often intentionally crafted for better or worse till death do you part again.

I was not ready to accept the fact that my "soul mate," Vita, intended a real-life changing interaction by foiling premeditated providence interruption when I opened Pandora's Box. I brought to life a past memory that could remain real and alive in my current life in this time and space via a loophole in the preprogrammed "destiny scheme."

Destiny is only a "suggestion," a perimeter for souls to move through, mostly unconsciously to the fact their lives are managed and controlled by external forces who are often family and acquaintances on the other side of life.

Sixteen-year-old Vita, a memory in my head with a shard of a soul, wished to do that, throw a kink into destiny with my help. I had no desire to do that, remain at the age of fifteen and grow up from there, and create other possible unforeseen bundles of scenarios and constituent consequences. The moment that thought entered my mind, Milton chimed in and said he would not allow such a situation to happen due to my circumstances while employed by him to perform the project I was involved with." So not to worry," said Milton. "That would disrupt the order of the universe! Michael." And Milton laughed.

Vita was under the influence of an adolescent mind and only a sliver of that mind and didn't grasp the implications of the situation. During that episode, I wasn't much wiser either. Is why Milton chimed in. Nevertheless, the experience opened to me just how entwined souls are through the centuries and forever in the fabric of many lives spent together.

At some point, we both ended up in this star system and on planet Uranus, where Vita and I were intimate friends with Neppti. Vita took on other assignments on other planets many Earth years before Neppti shipped off to Earth and was soon followed by me.

Neppti and I were not allowed to interact openly while on Earth this go-around other than infrequent episodes inside of Milton's ship and a few terse encounters on various moons and planets. Memories remain hidden concerning most interactions Neppti, and I experienced on Earth. A few of those encounters did reveal themselves during my assignment and involvement with Vita on the ship today. But the Gnokki considered those encounters unsuitable and removed them from the journal of material allowed in this book.

HYBRID BODIES HAVE NO HEART

Hybrids had a simple organ structure inside their bodies like nothing that would make sense if compared to human anatomy. No blood, no heart, no pancreas or liver but different versions, one small lung, short intestine, a larger sized human-type stomach, a bladder, and a few other body parts that humans don't have and fewer body parts than humans overall. No reproductive organs in the Hybrid male and female bodies, which are both impotent and not designed for child creation.

Hybrids are nothing like the highly complex human system with many inferior body parts that fail and are subject to manifold illnesses and defects throughout the human lifespan. Hybrid body parts never fail, and never became diseased and last for the duration the occupant wanted to remain inside of the hybrid body.

Hybrids destined to utopian colonies, and of this type and breed had no bellybuttons, the umbilical cord detached from inside the rectum cavity at some point after birth. Hybrid bodies lasted the equivalent of hundreds and even thousands of years without aging further than the prescribed age at the time and place of manufacture.

Food entered a Hybrid mouth that is lined with billions of taste buds, which allowed Hybrids to savor the food in ways humans could never imagine.

"The indescribable pleasure is intense but enigmatic to those without the equipment to taste the food at its core of deliciousness." Said the Gnokki.

Meaning that I, a human, could not imagine what I was missing when it came to the true taste of food because I lacked the equipment (hybrid taste buds).

Food entering the stomach is broken down into a mush down to the atomic level. The slush of atoms entered another chamber-organ and ignited into a flash of pure energy that energizes the Hybrid's electrical system for the human equivalent of several hours, days, and weeks with residual effects lasting much longer. After the energy spark from the food is absorbed, what remained was the ash-waste, which clumped into pellets and dropped from the anus out of the Hybrid body.

Hybrids are complex physiological electrical machines far more than human bodies but close enough to human physiology that humans can give birth to various types of Hybrids. Especially when the birth itself is an illusion and distraction to the reality of the birthing process supposedly taking place inside of Alien ships.

"In other words, what humans see with their eyes, and comprehend with inferior 3D minds, and the five inferior senses is not what really happens only an approximation of the hybrid birth." Recapped the Gnokki, sounding robotically from inside the handbag.

DOWNWARD SPIRAL

A few Hybrids had morbid desires to move downwards to medieval and barbaric planets such as Earth after luxuriating in utopia the equivalent of thousands of years. Having existed for lengthy periods in the lap of utopic luxury skewed their minds into believing they could bring change and help humans trapped in ego-driven hateful societies on planets like Earth. Overlooking the fact that they "themselves" had developed an ego, which drove them to believe they had powers that they didn't own or have but borrowed from the universe. They believed their advanced wisdom was the key. The catch, they were warned, was that entering the human zone required they forfeit much of their "borrowed knowledge advantage" and become like the animals known as humans.

These "star children" would receive tidbits of information via abductions but faced losing their way consumed in the muck of "human ego," which ultimately leads to ignorance, envy, greed, and hate. Warnings didn't faze those who had made up their minds to venture back into hell, from whence they had once existed, for the hell of it.

Having completely forgotten the complexities and realities existing on lower level planets was a flaw intentionally created by superbeings to inject nonviolent souls back into the soup kitchens of hellbent planets.

Souls of that caliber had the right to make egotistical choices. And that is the rub, intentional traps that less-than-perfect Hybrid souls and other types of beings continue to fall into, which keeps the planetary pots stirred with a lively variety and mix of souls.

Former utopic souls had little if any family back on Earth to save, help or provide counsel to, due to the fact they had been away from Earth thousands of Earth years and their linage dried up or diluted to the point they were no longer family. Likely they would encounter lost souls that belonged to family eons ago who haven't been able to escape the reincarnation cycles known as Hades. Such long-abandoned souls have exhausted their soul force (energy) with little meat on the soul-bones left to salvage, and not enough substance recognizable as family.

Decisions to move down rather than up came with other hidden hazards and snares. Family members higher up the ladder could be drawn down into the muck of hellish planets should they feel the need or the urge to come back to try and save the juvenile, naïve, gullible, but loveable souls.

DEMON WORLD

Demon worlds, one or more of the planets in each star system, boil over like a festering cauldron with never a break for the inhabitants of hell. Every star system has at least one such planet, some have several. They are horrendous places, and from where I made a few visits during my various assignments through the years with Milton. I encountered many souls stuck like flies on flypaper, trapped and tormented night and day, day and night, some for eternity. Most damned souls are clueless and not aware they are in such horrid places...distracted by illusions of simple pleasures created by demons to keep souls in the muck of self-importance.

Demons not of the biblical variety but far more sinister, devious, selfish, hateful tormenters of souls of every stripe, including human souls who have joined the ranks of demons. Humans recruited and snagged by their own evil deeds and egotistical desires for creating mischief in other people's lives. They are tormented souls placed into the flesh of humanoids and of humans, physical bodies where souls are inserted at birth and punished from the first minutes of existence until death relinquishes them back into the cosmos...for a time until like a boomerang's inevitable return.

Numerous spirit beings eagerly and dutifully wait to capture freed souls, released by the death of their physical bodies, and unclaimed by higher beings. The apprehended wretched souls are taken to other stations in the galaxy from where they are picked through by scavengers at a landfill, strewn with garbage and sorted and fought over as scraps. Salvageable souls are processed back into physical lives to be tested for latent value.

Demon planets are useful to the star systems they inhabit, by sucking up discarded and lost souls that have drifted out into space after dying on various planets and moons in star systems. Most souls are taken directly to their next regeneration ports from where they are assigned new lives, returned to where they came from, or sent to other places to undergo additional processing.

Lost souls are those that have fallen through the cracks for any number of reasons, abandoned by spirit guides is one of the justifications. When souls continually fail and ignore advice and direction from soul guides, guides abandon the souls, cut them free to drift out into space indefinitely. There are other reasons that souls lose their way and become festering pots of evil known only to the souls themselves who have become deluded by envy, greed, and false piety.

Lost souls wander aimlessly in space, and some get snagged inside the planets, moons, caves, oceans, abandoned buildings, basements, and end up claiming and then haunting wherever they end up residing. Attachments from previous lives and horrid situations are a small percentage of ghosts and hauntings. Most poltergeists have accidentally stumbled on where they are at any given time, and most don't know where they are, how they got there, or where they go next.

Lost souls can enter human babies in places around Hades (Earth) that are undesirable hellholes, where lives are extremely difficult and challenging when entered. Many babies born in such places have a gap, a few days before souls are placed into them, which allows lost souls opportunities to jump back into the physical world on their own if they so choose to (they are allowed).

But lost souls don't want back into the physical realm at lower levels and prefer to hide until captured by spirit beings, demons, headhunters, and other kinds of soul trackers. Bounty hunters and such are on the lookout for entertainment, tormenting opportunities, and cosmic rewards, which provides a slow road to potential recovery for the lost and abandoned souls.

Forsaken souls enter the phantom zones in steady streams, having died or executed on the hundreds of moons and planets in the star system. There is always a shortage of live human bodies to place the overflow of lost souls into, and therefore souls drift until a warm body presents itself in the form of a human type body, a tame animal, or a wild beast.

Normally, human bodies are specifically designed and created for the souls that will inhabit the body, human or otherwise. Nevertheless, supplementary human bodies, once born, mostly in undeveloped countries, planets, and moons, are allowed to become a refuge for rogue and abandoned souls. Auxiliary corporal bodies are created to sponge up lost souls and provide them a resting place.

The only way out of Hades is through the human body. Born into the human body and going through the crap thrown at the soul by demons and other type tormenters. Those who can handle the crap and manage to move forward will eventually break free, and for some, permanently escape demon-possessed hell-hole planets until they chose to return.

Souls are not equal in any way, shape, or form on demon worlds (Earth-type planets) or anywhere else in the universe. Naive souls have deluded themselves in believing such tripe. Many souls on Earth are working off minor infractions from previous lives and will move up to the higher cosmic ground after death.

CHAPTER 7

VENUS

Planet Venus is a sister Hade's planet with Earth, where many souls are taken to, from Earth, and from Venus to Earth for specialized treatments. Souls that consistently fail to move up from Earth often find themselves on Venus. Not that souls moving downward would have the wherewithal to know that or know much of anything during their existence on hades planets.

I was tasked by Milton to fetch a few souls from Earth and Venus and take them to the utopia colony and place them into Hybrids. Such souls have broken the chains that entangle and keep souls from advancing to higher places in the cosmic wonderland.

One of the souls I captured was named Fred. Fred died of old age. He was 92 and lived a difficult life but was about to receive his reward. His life was problematic due to his previous life, the one before this one. Fred was a soldier in a war zone, conscripted, and became a good soldier. Fred followed orders and performed assignments admirably. Towards the end of his career, having risen through military ranks, Fred became arrogant and mistreated people under his command, ordered them to do unsavory things to captured enemy soldiers.

During "this life," Fred avoided military duty, had no stomach for it, and the gods, his spirit guides, steered him away from becoming a soldier. A common practice in the mortal world, where most people (souls) are not placed into war situations twice in a row having served or been caught up in the horrors of war in a previous life.

Fred married his high school sweetheart, Rita, and had four children with her. Fred worked as a welder, long hours, and dirty hard work. Came home tired and mad nearly every day of his working life until he retired at the age of sixty-two. Fred couldn't make ends meet and had to find part-time work at a warehouse, where he drove a forklift during the night shift.

Fred's wife, Rita, left him years before he retired, having fallen in love with a man that she worked with at her job in a large office complex as a manager. After twelve years of a rocky marriage, Fred and Rita split up and divorced. His three sons and one daughter, who he raised without Rita's help, didn't get along with him, they blamed Fred for the divorce, for driving their mother away due to his obsessive grumpiness. Fred didn't drink, smoke, or do drugs but was plagued with a bad temper and attitude, the cross laid on him for his dirty deeds in his previous life as a soldier. None of Fred's children graduated high school, and eventually, as they got older one by one, drifted away and never again contacted Fred, their father (part of Fred's KARMA).

Fred was now in a nursing home, dying alone, abandoned by family and friends. Down deep inside, Fred was a good soul, but he had to pay the price for the deeds he committed during his previous life as a soldier gone rogue.

His four children and his wife, and so too the man she ran off with, were soldiers and family members of the soldiers under Fred's command during his previous life who did dirty deeds willingly while under Fred's command. Restitution was completed in this life for Fred. Fred was now free to move to a better life in the utopian colony, and I was there to harvest his soul from his dying wretched body.

Years earlier, Fred was abducted by Aliens, and his soul stripped out of his human body, temporarily, and placed inside a Hybrid's body. While on the ship Fred the Hybrid, mated with a Venusian woman abducted from Venus, named Sally. For the type of Hybrid that Fred was destined to become, personal, and physical contact was required. Fred had been abducted several times during this life on Earth, and so too was Sally, the Venusian woman, and they formed a bond over the years. Most of that information was blocked from both Fred and Sally, but they did remember many things in their dreams about each other during their escapades while inside an Alien ship.

Fred and Sally are soul mates that have shared several past lives together going back hundreds of years, and this was a reunion of sorts, but only for the duration of the Hybrid child, they were making together. Afterward, Sally returned to Venus to continue with her life, and she and Fred would not connect for hundreds of years in some future encounter where they might cross paths and entwine dependent on decisions along the way that they both make.

Sally became pregnant with Fred's boy child a decade earlier from today and gave birth to a Hybrid. That Hybrid was taken to the utopian colony ten years ago and is one of the thousands of soulless Hybrids running loose in the rainforest that has undergone rapid growth and was now the equivalent of 25 Earth years old.

I traveled to the nursing home, where Fred was wasting away. Fred resided there for eight years, put there by the state, because no family member claimed Fred or took care of him and his affairs after he had fallen ill. Fred was frail and barely hanging on to life. There was no one in the room with Fred. An empty bed in Fred's room that belonged to a man that shared the room with Fred and passed away a week earlier was empty. The bed had not yet been reassigned to another patient.

Family pictures in Fred's room were absent, with no flowers and not much of anything that would make the room a cheerful place. The room was dreary, depressing, and smelled of old age. My clothing from Milton's ship rendered me invisible, but it didn't matter, Fred was not awake or aware of me. Fred died in his sleep, and I grabbed his soul as it seeped out of his body and placed it directly into my handbag. I captured a few other souls in other places before making my way back to utopia inside of Milton's ship.

Back in the rainforest, I searched for Fred's offspring, the Hybrid Sally conceived, and gave birth after she and Fred consummated the transaction years prior. I found Hybrid-Fred roaming through the forest with animals and feeding on various plants near a brook. I called out to Fred's biological Hybrid by name, and he came over to me. I reached into my handbag and pulled out Fred's soul and placed it into Fred's Hybrid brain. Fred smiled, didn't say a word, and shot back into the forest like a jackrabbit. The Gnokki had prepared Fred with the details about his new life while he was a disembodied soul inside the handbag, and nothing further I needed to add to Fred.

Seductive caked-on lipstick of fake virtue worn by bogus angelic humans delivers the kiss of death to those unprepared and unworthy of truth.

BIRTH OF A HYBRID

Meg, the woman I witnessed giving birth to a Hybrid on the ship earlier that day, who became pregnant by a man she had met at a bar, had achieved a minimum level of integrity, which allowed her to live a far better life in her next incarnation. Meg's next incarnation is life as a Hybrid in the utopian colony on the outskirts of the Jovian planet. The man Meg met at the bar was not happenstance or coincidence but a planned encounter by the likes of cosmic worker bees.

"Many such encounters happen on ships like the one where Meg delivered her Hybrid child. And many happen in the human world from encounters in bars, churches, schools, workplaces, wherever people meet and end up engaging in sexual activity with the whoops factor, pregnancy. Or so they think, it's all planned right down to the sperm that will impregnate the egg and fertilize it with modified Alien DNA. Where and with whom it happens makes a difference, and there is a reason behind every contrived incident with human and Alien encounters." Exclaimed the Gnokki.

Meg was seduced by an Alien Hybrid from an unknown location nearby but not in the utopian colony. Meg's new life is programmed to happen in two Earth years from today. Meanwhile, Meg would live out her life as a human without having any clue what is in store for her shortly (a pre-arranged death).

"Soon after Meg dies, she will not be taken to higher places for a life-review as many (but not all) souls of people who die receive. Meg has surpassed her required merits and given a pass and will be taken directly to utopia and inserted into her Hybrid body that she gave birth to on the ship this morning." Said Milton.

Milton chimed in again and said, "you, Michael impregnated Meg on a Saturnian moon city outside the confines of the utopian zone. Meg's Hybrid child is the person Meg becomes on the utopian colony. After doing an interval in the confines of the utopian colony, Meg chose to become a citizen of the Uranus city under the name Neppti."

"Milton, that sounds absurd, and the timeline is out of whack and whacky, and I have no memory of that bizarre scenario. It's a manipulation of time to the level of irrational, unreasonable, and my mind gasps at the thought of it."

"Dimensional discombobulation" is what I call it, Michael, Said Milton.

"So, Milton, am I Neppti's father?" "No, Michael, your genes were used to create Meg's hybrid child, the hybrid body that Neppti used while in utopia." Claimed Milton.

Milton continued, "creating a hybrid is different than humans mating and having a child. A soul is not attached to a hybrid body as it is in a human body

199

(strapped in). Inside of a hybrid body is like wearing a loose-fitting leisure suit, plenty of legroom. A soul in a hybrid has more amenities, freedoms, and upgrades like living in a mansion, where a "human body comparable" is like living in a bungalow."

"Thanks, Milton, that explains everything (Sarcasm)." "What's 'legroom' got to do with all that other crazy stuff you been throwing at me all this day, Milton?" Nothing, Michael, just chit-chat."

"By the way, Michael, Neppti is the Hybrid's mother, and gave birth to the Hybrid that Neppti will live inside of two years from now." Which, by the way, the two years have already come and gone, as I mentioned earlier and Neppti has been living a Hybrid life on utopia for some time now. But here's the kicker, Neppti will not go to Uranus this time."

"How is that possible, Milton?" I asked. "No, please don't answer....!"

"Much of Meg's life is a fabrication masking the clandestine operation she volunteered for when Meg (Neppti) came to Earth from Uranus. As is much of your life on Earth, Michael." Said Milton.

I snapped back, "Milton stop answering from Uranus!" "I know you don't have an anus, Milton, but can't you ever give straight answers?" No answer from Milton.

MISSION ACCOMPLISHED

I'm back at my desk, and I look up at the clock on the wall, it says 3:00 AM only one hour passed, the snow out the window is coming down and accumulating rapidly as it was when I left the house that morning. I told Milton that one hour wasn't much time to do all the things I did today.

Milton responded, "you didn't even spend one hour working in utopia you spent the hour in my ship shooting the breeze with me, we had some good laughs, too bad you don't remember, you were quite the chatterbox, Michael. And by the way, my ship never moved from above your house the whole time, so put that in your pipe and smoke it, Michael."

I said back to Milton, "I don't own a pipe."

Milton responded, "if you want that one hour back, let me know, Michael."

"That makes no sense, as usual, Milton," I said.

About then, the Gnokki that dropped in before I was whisked up to Milton's ship that morning popped into view out of the woodwork of my office, the four that traveled with me and the four that were left in my house as sentries. They scurried around like the Three Stooges (eight Stooges), banging on each other and cracking dumb jokes then vanished back up into Milton's ship in a whiff and a puff of sparks. The clock on the wall now said 2:00 AM. No lost time at all!

Milton chimed in and said, "are you happy now, Michael?"

I asked, "was it all a dream, Milton?" Milton said, "no, my ship is a time cube and what happened, what took place this morning was something that happened a few years back and the things you remember, the few things, did happen today, but I will not tell you what they were otherwise they might go to your head, Michael. Time is a funny thing, a malleable thing easily manipulated by the Gnokki and me and by others like us. Good night, Michael, sweet dreams, and don't let the Gnokki bite."

"So, Milton, all the things I did was really done by the Gnokki?"

"Yes, Michael, you are like a 3-year-old helping mother make cookies in the kitchen."

BOOKS BY THE AUTHOR

In League with a UFO Second Edition (177 pages) ..1997

Shrouded Chronicles (267 pages) 2000

A Day with an Extraterrestrial (159 pages) 2006

An Italian Family, Capisce? (197 pages) 2011

Israel Crucified (215 pages) 2012

Orphans of Aquarius (209 pages) 2012

UFOs in the Year of the Dragon (217 pages) 2012

Mars and the lost planet Man (215 pages) 2014

Graduation into the Cosmos (203Pages)..................2016

Planet Eropmanop (252 pages) 2017

Alien hybrids and Nymphs of Jupiter (207 pages)....2019

BLOGS IN BOOK FORM

UFOs and Extraterrestrials are as real as the nose on your face Blog, 2005. Published in book form, 2011 (383 pages)

Coming clean on Extraterrestrials and the UFO Hidden Agenda...Blog, 2007-8

> (357 pages) Part 1...2011
>
> (329 pages) Part 2...2012
>
> (303 pages) Part 3...2012
>
> (329 pages) Part 4...2012
>
> (291 pages) Part 5...2013
>
> (351 pages) Part 6...2013

EXTRATERRESTRIAL SPEAK (2008-10)

PART ONE (347 pages) 2015

BOOK TWO (277 pages)   2016

PART THREE (263 pages). 2019

PART FOUR (355 pages)....2019

PART FIVE (233 pages).......2019

PART SIX (217 pages).........2019

WEBSITES

ufolou.com

baldin.proboards.com

FACEBOOK. Lou Baldini

Made in United States
Troutdale, OR
08/21/2024

22216943R00127